Against All Odds

He didn't even carry a gun, it wasn't necessary when he was so good with his fists. But after a fatal altercation with a proddy kid he began to see he was perhaps too good, especially as the boy had a mighty powerful father and brother who would be waiting for him when he was finally released from prison.

It seemed like the moment to start packing a gun – a very special kind of gun. He needed all the advantage he could get as he was only one man against many. Someone had to die to even up the odds.

Against All Odds

Hank J. Kirby

A Black Horse Western

ROBERT HALE · LONDON

© Hank J. Kirby 2012
First published in Great Britain 2012

ISBN 978-0-7090-9475-3

Robert Hale Limited
Clerkenwell House
Clerkenwell Green
London EC1R 0HT

www.halebooks.com

Typeset by
Derek Doyle & Associates, Shaw Heath
Printed and bound in Great Britain by
CPI Antony Rowe, Chippenham and Eastbourne

CHAPTER 1

SADDLETRAMP

He wasn't even packing a gun – not one that could be seen, anyway.

The glass of whiskey paused halfway towards his wide mouth as the unshaven ranny slightly behind him, who had spoken to him a few seconds ago, repeated his terse request:

'I said, move up and gimme some room.'

Still holding the whiskey, the taller man turned a sun-whipped face far enough to see the speaker, lowered his blue gaze to take him in.

'Talking to me, friend?'

'I ain't your friend and, yeah – I'm – talkin' – to – you!' The last five words were emphasized by a work-hardened finger poking the tall man in the chest: one – two – three – four – five!

The lean frame didn't give an inch under the pressure of the jabs and the voice that spoke was quiet, held in with an effort. 'Don't do that, friend.'

'*You talkin' to me?*' mimicked the range man. He looked along the bar at the thin line of drinkers and got a few smiles and maybe a chuckle in return.

One man even lifted his beer glass and said, 'You tell him, Crabbe!'

Encouraged, Crabbe said, 'Hey! I'm waitin'! I asked if you were talkin' to me – *friend?*'

And he started to poke again with the thick finger. '*One – two*—' That was as far as he got.

The tall man's left hand moved with the speed of a cat jumping a mouse and grasped the stiffened digit in a clamping vice. Crabbe howled and bent double almost going down to his knees.

'I asked you not to do that.'

Crabbe gritted big, smoke-stained teeth. 'Yeah? Well, how about . . . *this!*'

He whipped up his Colt from its holster. But it had barely cleared leather when there was an audible *crack!* in the suddenly quiet barroom. Crabbe went up to his toes, screeching, and then dropped in a dead faint, his finger dangling at a mighty awkward-looking angle. His head banged on the brass foot rail with a dull ring.

A murmur rippled along the bar and the scattered drinkers closed in for a better look at the now writhing Crabbe.

'What the hell you do that for?' demanded a barrel-chested man wearing stained range clothes, as tall as the gunless stranger but about seventy pounds heavier – all of it around the middle.

'You saw.'

'I seen you snap my pard's finger! How the hell's he gonna do ropin' and cowpunchin' now?'

'It'll heal.'

'What's he s'posed to do meantime? Starve?'

'No family, or friends to help him out?'

'Crabbe? Hell, even his hoss can't stand him!' said someone on the edge of the small crowd, who earned himself a laugh or two.

'I'll remember that, Danno!' the big-bellied man growled and then turned to the stranger.'Listen, you, you can't come in here and do what you just done and hope to get away with it.'

The tall man's eyebrows arched. 'I came in to enjoy a quiet drink, friend, not to "get away" with anything.'

'Is that so!' The big man stepped back and looked the other over.

He topped six feet by a couple of inches, but was lean with it. His plain grey shirt and well-faded brown corduroy trousers with their long legs, and dusty, scuffed boots, put him down as a saddletramp.

This, for some reason, gave the big man more confidence. And there were no signs of hidden guns or knives.

'Mister, I believe Crabbe asked you to make room at the bar for him. You din' do it.'

'He *told* me to make room.'

'Now *I'm* tellin' you!'

The tall man sighed. 'Friend, if you can't find room enough to hitch a foot over the rail and lean an elbow on the counter, you better start thinking about losing some weight – mostly round the middle, I'd say.'

There was abrupt, almost total silence again in the bar, eyes swinging between the big-bellied ranny and the easy-looking tall man in the grey shirt. The barkeep discreetly armed himself with a length of wood, keeping one hand below the counter top, lips pursed.

'You callin' me "fat"?' demanded the belligerent ranny, hand knocking a half-empty glass of beer on its side.

'I'll be calling you a lot worse'n that you don't buy me another beer to replace that one you just spilled.'

The big man's jaw dropped briefly. 'Buy you a drink? I'll buy you time in Boot Hill, *that's* what I'll do, you dumb bastard!

He swung a punch, wild and free, and telegraphing his intention all the way, like a charging buffalo. The tall man casually lifted his left arm, deflecting the blow smoothly. Then his right fist exploded in the middle of the big man's face.

Blood sprayed, cartilage crunched, teeth broke or loosened, and the big man staggered along the bar, scattering the gawking drinkers. Knees folding, his chin struck the edge of the bar before he spread out on the floor on his back, sawdust sticking to his bloody, mangled face.

The barkeep leaned across the counter, his length of wood waving about aimlessly. He jumped when the man in the grey shirt asked quietly, 'You aiming to use that?'

'Huh?' The 'keep dropped the length of wood hastily, stepped back and licked his lips. 'Er, listen, I'll pour you a drink – on the house.'

'Right kind of you.'

'What the hell you hit him with?' a man in the front row of gawkers asked. The tall man held out his right hand and they saw scars and bumps on the sun-dark skin.

'You holdin' a roll of dimes, or quarters?' asked the barman setting a glass of foaming beer on the counter.

The tall man turned his hand over and opened it. No roll of coins.

'Judas! That was one helluva punch!'

The tall man drank some beer. 'It's warm.'

'Sorry, but, er, mebbe you better do your drinkin' someplace else, huh?'

'If that's what you want. I'm looking for work. Point me in the direction of a job and I'll get outta your hair.'

The barkeep shrugged and started mopping up the bar. A man in the crowd said, 'I hear they're hirin'-on at that trail herd down on the flats. S'posed to've lost a couple fellers in a Injun raid somewhere down-trail.'

'That's Skip Barlow's outfit. He's got a good name,' someone else said.

The tall man shoved the unfinished beer towards the barkeep and straightened his weathered hat. 'I'll settle for that; I'm a peaceable man.'

9

As he walked towards the batwings, a voice said, 'If that's peaceable, I hope he's nowheres near me when he decides to get riled.'

Skip Barlow made a note against the name of the man he had just hired for his trail drive, stifled a yawn and looked up at the next applicant standing in front of the battered table he had set up in the shadow of the chuck wagon. 'Last one, eh? Mebbe it'll make you lucky.'

'I could cross my fingers.'

The tall man from the saloon slightly stooped towards the low table. Idly, he brushed dust from his clothes, clean but hanging a little loosely on his rangy frame and obviously old. He wore no gun rig and his hat was tilted forward to shade his face. What Barlow could see of it seemed on the thin side and the eyes looked steady enough. But Barlow put a deal of stock in being able to read a man's face, mostly using the eyes as a guide.

'Why cross your fingers?'

The tall man shrugged. 'You're picky. You've sent four men packing. That one you just wrote in was the first you've hired in an hour.'

'I'm picky, and you're sassy. I guess we don't need to waste each other's time.'

Barlow started to close his book as the other said, 'I've been standing in the damn sun for an hour. You owe me enough courtesy to let me say my piece.'

Barlow was a man in his fifties, trail-hardened and no-nonsense. His first reaction was to tell this ranny

10

to get the hell out but something made him hesitate.

'Tilt your hat back.'

'What?'

'So I can see your face.'

'It's not on any dodger if that's your idea.' As he spoke the man thumbed back his hat and let it sit on the back of a head of fairly short fair hair. There were scars above both eyes and a thin one wriggling across his forehead. His nose had been on the wrong end of more than one fist, too, Barlow figured, noting the banged-up knuckles as well.

'Hell, I got no use for a brawler, friend. *Adios.*'

The man reached out as Barlow made to lift his book and pencils. The trail boss snapped his head up, mouth grim. 'Leave it!'

Calm blue eyes looked down into Barlow's deeply tanned face. 'I got those scars prize-fighting. I'm no drunken brawler.'

Barlow almost spat. 'Hell, you think that qualifies you for a job ridin' with my trail herd?'

'No, I'm just telling you I didn't get those scars from drunken brawls. I earned 'em the hard way, and it wasn't worth it.'

Barlow steadied, studied him more closely. There was some sort of intensity about this *hombre* that had him curious. 'Heard there was a bit of a scrap in the saloon earlier. . . . You?'

There was a hesitation but Barlow had a notion that when the man spoke, it was with truth. 'Yeah. Coupla rannies wanted to bully their way to the bar. I was in their way.'

'You got a name?'

'Matt Ronan.' It was said quielty, a little tautly.

The trail boss kept staring hard. 'Sure it's not "Rip" Ronan? Hellfire in the squared ring a while back?'

The calm blue eyes seemed colder now as the answer came flatly: 'I've been called that.'

'And a lot worse, I reckon. You done time for—'

'I've done it, that's the main thing. Now I'm free and looking for work. I know trail driving, had a small outfit of my own years ago. I need a job now and I'd like to hire on with you – you've got a good reputation. But if you're prejudiced, just say so and I'll quit wasting both our time.'

Barlow glared but held his temper. His voice was a little thick as he said, 'Pride can kill you, boy.'

'Is it quicker'n starving to death because you can't find work?'

'You tried for other jobs?'

'Seven.'

Barlow whistled. 'They all recognize you?'

'Only after I told 'em my name.'

'Judas' ghost, feller, you could've used another name.'

'My name's Ronan. I've been called others, but that's the only name I answer to.'

Barlow let out a long breath, gnarled fingers pinching his stubbled lower lip. 'How do I know you can ride herd?'

'Because I told you I could.'

'How come the prize-fightin'?'

'I needed extra money. It was a quick way to get a small stake.'

'Quick and . . . painful.' A big hand indicated the small nest of scars over those chill blue eyes.

'Pain passes. Look, I know there'll be others coming down here lookin' for work. A whole bunch were talking about it in the saloon; if they ever stop drinkin' they'll be along, so if I'm wasting my time, say so now and let me get on my way.'

Barlow's chair creaked as he sat back, thumbing back his own hat, shaking his head slowly as he looked into the rugged face of the man called Ronan.

'You're a hardcase, Ronan, I can see that. How long since you got outta jail?'

'Little over a month.'

'No work at all in that time?'

'Swamped a few bars, cleaned stables, dug a trash pit.'

'You're not fussy then.'

'I like to eat. Thanks for your time, Mr Barlow.'

He set his battered hat squarely on his head and started to turn away.

'Where the hell you think you're goin'? Don't you want a ridin' job after standing in the sun for so long?'

Ronan looked back over one shoulder, soberly. 'You gonna take a chance on me?'

'Is that what I'm doin'? Hell, I was hoping I was hirin' a good trail man.'

'You are. You hire me, Mr Barlow, and you'll get

your money's worth.'

'I damn well better.' Barlow opened his book again and picked up a pencil, holding it towards Ronan. 'Make your mark and grab your outfit and—'

'I'm wearin' my outfit.'

Barlow's heavy eyebrows arched. 'They all the clothes you got?'

'They've been in mothballs for three years and they don't pay you a wage on the chain gang.'

'Well, I guess we can find somethin' in the slop-chest that'll fit you. A horse comes with the job, and mebbe we can find you a gun.'

'I can take or leave guns. Fact, left two in trail towns gettin' here. So many guns around these days you can't get but a few bucks for 'em.'

Barlow grunted, frowning a little. 'You don't like guns, huh?'

'They're necessary, I guess. I'm obliged to you, Mr Barlow. I won't let you down.'

'I'm damn sure you won't.'

Barlow sounded very emphatic, almost . . . threatening.

It didn't seem to bother Ronan.

CHAPTER 2

WILD NIGHT

Wildfire started the stampede.

It streaked red, yellow and silver out of the dark bulbous sky pressing down on the mountain range alongside the trail to railhead.

There was a sizzle above the flatrock wall that protected the settling herd from the promised rain. Hard on the sizzling sound came the *crack*! that bulged the eardrums of the trail drivers. Every man except the cook was mounted, endlessly riding – here, there and over yonder – wherever the steers were stirring restlessly, unable to settle, sensing the building storm as night closed in.

It had been a long, hard drive up this new trail, and it had all the signs of being a long, hard night. When the lightning struck the rim of the wall, shattered rock exploded outwards and fell amongst the herd, That was all it took: they were up and bawling and snorting and horn-tossing within seconds of the flash of blinding light that followed the strike. Then came the first of the raindrops: hard, driving, stinging. The combination was all that was needed to send the herd into a bawling, rushing panic.

Ronan looked swiftly towards the big steer with the murderous spread of horns that he had been watching on and off for some time: he sensed that if there was going to be trouble, it would start with this red-backed varmint with the splash of white smack in the middle of its spine like spilled paint. He was right. He saw the big, lolling eyes and the menacing rip of the horns as the animal cut loose with an ear-bending bellow and started to clamber over the backs of two smaller steers in front. One collapsed under the weight, the other wrenched aside, snorting, as the big one's hoofs tore bloody wounds in its hide.

Then the bighorn was clear, pawing the ground as the rain pelted with drops that stung like buckshot. Tossing lethal horns, the herd was away, gathering speed swiftly, surging and jostling.

Suddenly,the ground was trembling and Ronan's bellowed, '*Stampede!*' was almost lost in the increasing ruckus as the herd turned as one in the wake of the leader. Ronan wheeled his hardy little trail mount and spurred after the herd that seemed to rise like a section of the ground itself, and go lumbering after the line already crowding and jostling behind the steer with the big horns.

The men from early nightshift who had been drinking coffee around the cooking fire at the chuckwagon swore, scalded their mouths trying to finish their java, then tossed the tin mugs in the general direction of the wagon as they leapt to their stirrups.

The cook, Mr McRostie, let loose with a stream of curses that drained the breath from his 60-year-old lungs, and began gathering his gear, kicking out the fire. He tossed the utensils into the back of the chuckwagon and ran for the driving seat: he knew damn well these rannies wouldn't return here to the campsite once they'd run down the herd and brought it to a stop. It meant he would have to chase the stampede in the lumbering wagon and be damn well expected to have coffee ready – and fresh biscuits if he knew the appetites of this trail crew with their bottomless bellies. He grunted, swayed up into his seat and picked up his long-handled whip, the team already nervous, but ready.

Riders tore past the wagon ignoring the shouting, cursing cook, concentrating on the snorting, *cussed* damn steers that were building into a fine old speed, pounding hoofs scattering clouds of gritty mud.

Why did the worst stampedes always happen at night!

Ronan half-rose in the stirrups, leaning towards the arched neck of his racing mount, bent leg muscles aching and screaming as they took his shifting weight while he manoeuvred through the outskirts of the thundering mob, gaining slowly on the leader. Other riders were starting to crowd the steers at the edge, forcing them back, the herd beginning to wedge up, but still showing no signs of slowing. A few gunshots cracked into the wet air but didn't seem to have any effect.

Ronan had been given a Colt and a Winchester by Barlow but he left the weapons in leather, fighting his way along the edges, wrenching the reins and hauling the mount beyond the raking tips of the long-horns. The cowpony knew its job well and with only mild hesitation it skimmed past the grunting cows, their snorts sending ribbons of snot from the dis-tended nostrils flying to mix with the rain.

Ronan's horse suddenly whinnied and jumped away as horns drew blood across the left side of its chest. He fought for control, got it, kicked the steer, the leader now, behind the ear and gave it another under the jaw for luck.

But it was bad luck, because the steer broke from the edge, floundered, and horned the pony, though not deeply, across its rippling chest. It whistled shrilly in pain and veered sharply enough to almost unhorse Ronan. He righted himself and made his decision as the big steer drew slightly ahead of the front line of its followers.

He drew his Colt, rammed the bleeding, reluctant, yet obedient, cowpony into the side of the steer, leaned far out of the saddle, rain stinging his face, and shot it between the eyes.

It dropped in its tracks and Ronan wrenched the cowpony aside almost by physical force, the reins drawing so tight he figured they might even snap.

When the big steer fell, it sprawled, right in front of the following line. Some cows stumbled, bawling, rearing, causing confusion and one hell of a noise and there began a pile-up when they failed to dodge the downers. Ronan got out of the way as some steers crashed and others twisted aside, starting to turn, but too sharply. They crossed the line of mindless animals behind, met the thundering beasts, in another mêlée and a racket that could have come from the pits of hell itself.

Cattle scattered, wrenching away from the pile-up, leaving space enough for the hard-riding cowboys to weave between, to cut out small bunches that might still have had the notion to continue running. They scattered the herd as well as they were able so the fear of some could not communicate to others and set them off in yet another stampede. The struggling pile bawled piteously.

After long minutes, they began to settle and the riders started amongst them, weaving in with rope ends and kicks and many, many swear words. Luckily, the mad run had stopped on decent grassland, and in a surprisingly short time most of the hard-breathing bovines were chomping away contentedly, hemmed in by the weary, drenched riders.

'Let's go get some hot java!' suggested one ranny at the top of his voice, and was cheered for it. Then someone let out a wild yell.

'Goddamnittohell! McRostie's crashed the chuck-wagon!'

It was one hell of a mess. Skip Barlow surveyed the upturned vehicle amidst the spilled foods and gear. The team had managed to twist free but one horse hobbled on three legs and was destined for a quick bullet.

Mr McRostie was huddled at the base of a bush, dazed and bleeding. Barlow signed for two cowboys to take care of him, took off his hat and scratched at his bald scalp.

'Hell, one of the new Studebaker wagons, too, with all the food drawers built in, even a place for the outfit's sleepin' gear. Cost me over eighty bucks. Now look at it. Be lucky to get a lousy dollar for it.'

The rain gathered strength and drenched the weary men. The herd was still restless but under control, wet backs gleaming in an occasional lightning flash.

'It don't look so good right now, but it can be put together,' Ronan said, earning himself a hard, sceptical stare. 'I was wagon boss with the prize-fightin' outfit before they saw me in a fight and decided to put me on their boxing team. We travelled by wagon, town to town. An oldtimer showed me how to fix wrecks – and we had plenty, the way some of 'em drove.'

'And you reckon you can put that mess together?'

'Might look kinda patched-up, but, yeah, I reckon I can get it movin' again and good enough for Mr McRostie.'

'One front wheel's all buckled, spokes busted,' spoke up Cannon, one of the point riders. 'Axle's bent to hell and gone, too.'

Ronan's mouth tightened. 'Mebbe spoke too soon – I'm no wheelwright. Could likely improvise on the rear wheels, but the front axle needs an expert.'

There were disappointed murmurs from the gathered men but Ronan got them to work collecting the bits and pieces of the wagon, searching the mess for tools to work with, muscling the damaged frame across and planning the reconstruction.

By daylight, it looked like a chuckwagon again – even if a mite on the rough side – but only the rear wheels were fitted, the front assembly resting on a log.

The wrangler, a short fiesty man who never said much, had been sent on ahead to scout. He returned to find lousy coffee – Mr McRostie not feeling so good yet – and cold biscuits for breakfast. But when Barlow asked for his report, he yawned and outdid himself by making what was, for him, a speech. He gestured to the mountain range, bulking dark and wet through the rain. 'Met a local rancher on his way home after a wingding and he says there's a town on t'other side called Skywater. There's a pass up ahead leads to it. Probably get that front wheel fixed there, Skip. River's up after the rain, anyway, an' no crossin' point for at least five miles upstream. We'll have to wait for a day or two before we try to push the herd across.'

'Better watch it, Spurs! You're gonna have a sore throat from all that talkin'!' a cowboy said and there was a guffaw. The wrangler said abruptly,

'I've said my piece. Do what you like.'

He stomped off, narrow shoulders squared aggressively and cowboys who towered over him and easily out-weighed him moved aside quickly to let the can-tankerous wrangler through.

'I hope this Skywater's big enough to have a good wheelwright,' Ronan said. 'I mean, a twisted front axle's no easy thing to set straight; there're bearings to align and so on.'

Barlow gave up trying to light his pipe, even with the bowl inverted, and stuffed it in his sodden shirt pocket as he said, 'I've heard of Skywater. Pretty big for a town out this way.' He glanced around. 'Any you fellers been there?'

'I have. Lived with a woman there for a nigh on a year until—' The speaker, a bearded rider, stopped when Barlow snapped,

'Never mind your love life, Butch! What about the town? It got a wheelwright or not?'

'As I recall, yeah. Good one, too – name of Cline.'

Barlow pursed his lips and began to nod slowly: 'Yeah, I've heard the name. . . .' He broke off as he saw Ronan's face, taut and thin-lipped. He frowned.

'Cline?' Ronan echoed hoarsely, turning to Butch. 'Jesse Cline?'

Butch said, 'Think so. Runs the wheelwright busi-ness and a big ranch, too, with one of his sons, Denby. Was another son but he got killed somewhere up north years ago.'

Ronan looked mighty thoughtful and Barlow asked quietly, 'You know this Jesse Cline, Matt?'

Cold blue eyes swung towards him slowly.

'No.'

Barlow straightened. 'Mmmmm, well, you do

know somethin' about wagon wheels. You'd better ride with me in the buckboard and we'll take the busted wheel in and see how long he'll be fixin' it.'

Ronan's face was expressionless as he said slowly. 'Whatever you say.'

Barlow continued to stare. 'The herd can be restin' while we get the wheel fixed. I'll have to replace some of the stores that got destroyed by the rain and the crash, too. This damn delay's gonna cost plenty before we're through.'

Matt Ronan nodded without enthusiasm. 'You're the boss.'

'I am,' Barlow confirmed shortly, hard-eyed, as Ronan turned away towards one of the drag riders who was tending the horn gouges on the chest of Ronan's cowpony.

'Looks like you better find me another mount, Spurs. This one's gonna have to rest a spell.'

The wrangler grunted as Ronan scratched the injured horse behind one ear.

Skip Barlow watched silently, wondering why Matt Ronan had lied to him about knowing Jesse Cline. . . .

This trip to Skywater could prove to be a lot more interesting than he had figured.

CHAPTER 3

TRAIL TO SKYWATER

The buckboard clattered out of the narrow pass and a panorama of mountains and sky spread out before them.

Ronan was driving while Barlow fought to keep his pipe alive and puffing, bracing knees and thighs against the seat sides as the buckboard slid around the bends. Their two mounts were tethered to the tailboard and not happy at eating so much dust. But Barlow was a belt-and-braces man and refused to travel into unknown territory without back-up mounts, which was, of course, the wise thing to do.

In the tray, the broken wheel and the twisted axle thudded and bounced as they hit bumps in the trail.

There had been little conversation but when Skip Barlow finally got his pipe drawing to his satisfaction, he puffed a lungful of blue smoke and said,

'You never went far with the prize-fightin'?'

'Professional, you mean? Nah, not disciplined enough. I had a helluva punch – still have – if I get the chance to land it just right, but the pros don't give away many chances like that. It was good enough to make me "star" of the tent show and that was about it.'

'Spud Gulbranson's, wasn't it? Recall him workin' the frontier for years with his troop of "unbeatable" prizefighters. All these tough-lookin' *hombres* lined up on a plank outside the big tent, makin' snide remarks about the "quality" – or lack of it! – of the locals; Gulbranson offering five crisp dollar notes if anyone could go three rounds with their top fighter, which I guess was you?'

Ronan nodded, a touch of nostalgia beginning to show on his wind-burned face. 'Yeah, tough man, Spud. Led me on a mite, tellin' me he'd see about getting me into professional prize fights and make me rich – he'd be my manager, of course. Never came to anything. Fights were mostly with stooges planted in the audience: they'd shout insults at us fighters up on the board and we'd make out we were mad and throw out the "challenge", make it sound like a genuine grudge match. Was all a set-up, but it gave the paying customers their money's worth. Now and again we'd let the stooge win.' Ruefully he added, 'Occasionally we didn't have any choice!'

Barlow nodded and they rode for almost another mile, coming to a winding trail down a steep slope.

While he cleaned his pipe bowl Barlow said, trying to sound casuals, 'You had some trouble, as I recall.'

Ronan concentrated on getting the vehicle down the rest of the narrow trail and didn't answer until they were on a level stretch, with the suggestion of buildings way up front, hazy against another low line of hills.

All he said was, 'Some.'

Barlow waited. Nothing more forthcoming. 'Boy died, didn't he?' Ronan nodded and the trail boss couldn't keep from probing some more. 'Always remembered the name, Fighting Farley, wasn't it?'

'That was the name he used.' Ronan spoke curtly, barely audible.

'Heard he used to play stooge for Gulbranson. Someone said his real name was . . .' he paused, not sure whether he should go on. 'Ah, never mind. I guess that's your business. Thing I found queer was that the kid got your back up so easy. I mean, I read about the trial and you said he made you mad as a hornet, but you refused to say how.'

After a while, when the trail boss was sure Ronan wasn't going to answer, the man said, 'Kept calling me seven kinds of bastard.'

Barlow actually jumped, snapped his head around, frowning. 'Well, that ain't the most flatterin' name to call a man, but to make you so mad you near tore his head off his shoulders. . . !'

Ronan slowed the vehicle and turned to look steadily into Barlow's face. 'Happens I am a bastard, in the truest sense of the word.'

Skid Barlow half choked on a throatful of pipe smoke, went through some mild curses and tapped out the dottle on the edge of the seat. 'Well, I dunno how I'd act if it was me, but seems you might've been just a mite . . . too techy.'

'I was killin' mad,' Ronan said flatly. 'That tag's bedevilled me all my life: "You no-good little bastard!" "What the hell else would you expect from a snotty-nosed bastard like you," that kinda stuff. Same sort of talk killed my mother, shamed her into her grave, after scrubbin' floors and doing the "better" folks' laundry. Never knew my old man and she never mentioned his name. I was seven years old when she died.'

'Hell! Who took care of you?'

'Me.'

'What! A 7-year old? You fed an' clothed yourself? Aw, come on, there must've been someone to help you.'

'Yeah, some good folk now and again would give me a feed, let me sleep in the barn, even hang some of their own kid's worn-out clothes on a part of the wash line where I could snitch 'em at night: didn't want to be seen helping me out.' He drove looking straight ahead, mouth in a tight line. ' 'Course it bein' such a Christian town – they had signs that said so: *You are now entering Mill River, a Christian town* – I was dragged to school when they could catch me and beat up when I got lessons wrong, generally kicked around. Ah, never mind that stuff. I wasn't the only one got the rough end of the cob, and you didn't have to be a bastard, either. Just different in some way from the norm.'

Barlow cleared his throat. 'This kind a thing went on for some time?'

'Those days and in that town it was expected, so I jumped a train when I was eight or nine and never went back. Tried not to think about it, but that preacher, he sent out notices for my return and twice they started to take me back, but I got away, and, well, somehow that damn "bastard" tag stuck with me, always came out.' He shrugged. 'Years of it wore me down and I got into a lot of fights, and was pretty good. Gulbranson spotted me and took me on his team. I liked it, bein' able to fight without bein' dragged off to jail or fined or something. Most times it was OK working ranches or trail herds, but now and again the name'd come up and—' He paused, looked Barlow straight in the eye. 'If you were going to say the boy I killed in that tent fight was named Farley Cline, you'd be right.'

The only sounds for the next half mile were the creaks and groans and thuds from the wagon, or the occasional snort of the sweating team, a whicker from the mounts behind.

'Now, you're not gonna blame Cline for the kid rilin' you, are you? Because if you aim to prod him into a fight, I'm gonna have to—'

Ronan smiled crookedly. 'I'll tell you why I want to see him. I want to tell him I'm sorry for killing Farley.'

Barlow's jaw dropped. 'My God! You are sure a

28

strange one, Ronan!'

'So I've been told a few times.'

'*Sorry*!'

'Yeah. Found out later Farley was tired of playing the stooge, wanted my place as top fighter of the team.' His voice hardened some then. 'Heard his old man encouraged him, made him feel kinda like he wasn't really good enough to do it, and somehow he found out just the thing to get me riled. I guess he hoped I'd make some mistakes, and the kid'd get the better of me and. . . .' he shrugged.

Barlow looked at him sharply. 'If I recollect right, it was Jesse got you sent to jail, wasn't it? Didn't he stir the hell outta everyone until they brought some sort of charges agin you – negligence or somesuch – that landed you in the pen?'

Ronan nodded.

'You gonna discuss that with him?'

'We'll see.'

'Well, I hope you've lost some of that hair-trigger temper then.' Barlow was serious, eyes hard, unrelenting. 'I don't aim to be a party to a killin', even inadvertently.'

'Like I said, we'll see.'

Skywater was a sprawling town, wide streets, plenty of space between houses and businesses. There was a kind of lake beyond, and the angle of the sun gave it a blue look, reflecting the sky and the hills. It looked almost like a painting and Ronan slowed the buckboard as they topped out on a rise. Both men took time to look at the scene.

'Guess that's why they call it Skywater,' opined Ronan.

Barlow nodded. 'Could be. This is the first time I've driven this trail to get to Dodge, never took time to learn much about the town. Some of the boys seem to think it's a good place for a wingding.'

'They'd think hell's foyer was a good place if there was enough booze and gals.'

Barlow smiled thinly. 'Yeah, but you and me are here on business.' He looked levelly at Ronan. '*My* business comes first; anything you want to do you can take care of after makin' arrangements about repairs to the wheel.'

'I know.'

'Let's get down and see what this Cline can do for us.'

The wheelwright's place was one street back from the main drag which was wide as a paddock and because of the space didn't seem crowded with the traffic; wagons, buggies, buckboards, riders, folk strolling casually through it all.

There was a subdued racket coming from the long low building that housed the wheel works: hammers on metal, the rattle of timber falling from a stack, men shouting. The office was near the street entrance and it was Jesse Cline himself who came to the door as Barlow and Ronan climbed down from the buckboard.

'Your vehicle rides well enough. Guess whatever repairs you want is something in the back?'

He was a large man, belly expanding now he was heading into his fifties, and he had a close-cropped snow-white beard. Some of the grey had reached up into his dark hair, even flecking his heavy eyebrows.

The eyes beneath were grey, the left one showing some milkiness of approaching vision problems, maybe a cataract. Those eyes looked over the new-comers very carefully. He introduced himself and thrust out a big hand towards Barlow.

The trail boss shook hands and said his name, gestured to Ronan, saying only, 'This is one of my point riders, Matt. He can tell you what we need done.'

Cline nodded curtly, briefly touching Ronan's hand, eyes piercing. 'What's the trouble?'

Ronan led the way to the tray, threw back the burlap that had been covering the broken wheel and bent axle. Cline looked at the damage professionally. 'Not too bad. S'pose you want it yesterday?'

Barlow smiled thinly. 'Would've been handy. How long will it take? I'm restin' my herd other side of the pass, waitin' for the river to go down.'

'It runs off pretty fast once the rain stops. I guess I could have this ready by late tomorrow?'

'That'll be fine. We'll camp out in the buckboard by your lake. Looks good.'

'Uh-huh,' Cline said, studying Ronan closely. He got a blank stare in return, then finally said, 'You've changed some.'

'Try a few years on the chain gang. You'd change, too.'

Barlow was mighty tense now, not quite knowing

31

what to expect from these two facing off so abruptly.

'Should've been ten years – or a rope.'

'You made that clear at the trial.'

'You come here to make trouble?'

Ronan shook his head. 'Matter of fact when I heard you were the wheelwright I decided to come tell you – tell you I'm sorry about what happened to Farley.'

Jesse Cline's face was hard and rugged now, the eyes slightly slitted. 'Sorry? That does a lot of good.'

'I . . . lost my temper. But the prison doctor told me it wasn't my punch that killed the boy, it was him hitting his head on that damn low metal turnbuckle on the corner post of the ring. Gulbranson was s'posed to've had it covered.' He paused. Cline seemed to straighten some, his brow creasing. 'He said you were told that before the trial.'

'Was your punch drove him into the turnbuckle!'

'Now, look, gents . . .' Barlow said, clearing his throat. 'All this is water under the bridge and no good can come from pawin' over it now.'

They didn't even seem to be aware of the trail driver's presence, stood with bleak gazes locked.

'You're "sorry"!' gritted the wheelwright.

'I'll be honest with you, took me a long time before I decided I was sorry. Up until then, all I wanted to do was punch *your* face in.'

Jesse Cline stiffened noticeably and his frown deepened. 'You aren't gonna salve your conscience this easy, you son of a bitch!'

Ronan spread his hands. 'Well, I've told you how I

feel, and I mean it. Now I'll just wait with the boss till the front wheel's ready and—'

'Might be best if you go back to the herd, Matt,' Barlow broke in quickly, shooting a sidelong glance in Cline's direction. 'I can handle the buckboard now we've seen what the trail's like.'

'No point in me leaving now, boss. It'll be dark before I get through the pass.'

'Half-moon right now,' Cline said casually, but with a hard edge to his words he apparently was unable to hide.

Ronan pursed his lips. 'I think I'll stay, boss.'

Barlow was decisive now. 'No, you get on back. Jonesy hurt his back durin' the stampede and Yorkey on point has a bad horn gash in his left leg. The herd'll still be edgy so we need all the men on nighthawk we can get.'

'All right, boss,' Ronan said reluctantly. 'Or I could stay and bring back the wheel and axle when it's finished and you could ride on to the herd and fix things to your liking.'

Barlow almost smiled. 'Maybe we'll flip a coin.'

'Look, you two argue your business someplace else,' Cline cut in heavily. 'This is my office. I've said I'll have your wheel assembly ready tomorrow and I'm a man of my word. You go settle your problems elsewhere.'

Barlow nodded and Ronan shrugged. Jesse Cline turned away from his office door and walked down into the work area where the hammering had started up again. They dimly heard him call to one of the men above the clatter and a furnace heating iron for a wheel rim suddenly roared and blasted a sheet of flame. The smell of hot charcoal was overpowering.

Ronan followed Barlow to the street door and they unhitched the team and their mounts, led the animals down the street towards the livery.

'What's your worry, boss? Think I'm gonna have trouble with Cline?'

'Not only think it; I think you're lookin' forward to it. You gonna remind him it could be seen as his fault? Eggin' the kid on to try and beat you?'

'No, I am sorry the kid died; he hit his head when he fell, but Jesse's right. It was my punch that knocked him down.'

'You had cause from what you've told me.'

'At the time, I've had years to think about it since.'

Barlow glanced back towards the wheel workshop. 'So's Cline.'

CHAPTER 4

NIGHT RIDERS

Night came early in the pass, it being so narrow and high-walled.

The deep shadow, with a hard edge of coolness, washed quickly through the winding cutting. Ronan figured he wasn't more than halfway when he came to a bend and caught a glimpse of a small rockpool. He decided to camp right there.

He had his bedroll, hardtack, some coffee – and Barlow had slid a Winchester into the empty saddle scabbard without comment before he had left town. He smiled thinly: wasn't such a bad idea at that.

He made a small camp-fire, brewed some coffee that could have doubled for drain cleaner and made his jaws ache chomping on strips of jerky that every trail driver carried in the bottom of his saddle-bag. Above, a handful of stars were brilliant jewels on a velvet background, and he lay back, propped against his bedroll and watched them as he smoked.

Well, it hadn't been the wisest move coming to see Cline, he allowed, but he had hoped the man might be over some of his bitterness by this time. And Ronan himself had needed to tell Jesse he was sorry about Farley's death.

The kid had been one of those aggravating, spoiled brats who was more than a youth, but not quite a man. And being a Cline he had been well used to having his own way – and no redress about his actions or how he spoke to people.

No getting away from it, Farley Cline had made him good and mad, (like he did most folk he met) and he had damn well known he was doing it, deliberately trying to prod Ronan into a rage so he could cry 'foul' and win Gulbranson's bonus.

Hell with it! It was years ago now and he'd told Jesse how he felt – *genuinely* felt. He didn't seem any easier about it but it was just something he knew he *had* to do.

And he knew now Barlow was right: Cline wasn't going to let it rest there!

At the moment he decided to jack a shell into the Winchester's breech, he heard the trickle of gravel on the far bend of the wall that rose in front of him. He rolled quickly to the right, snatching the rifle as the gun on the wall blasted, its muzzle flame tearing the night apart enough so he could see projecting rocks and even a small tuft of grass growing. He also caught the edge of a dark face and the frayed brim of a hat with sweat stains on the crown.

Ronan was on his belly now, sweeping the Winchester around as the man triggered again. The bullet whined off the wall above him and his rifle answered before the gunflash across the bend had died. He heard a grunt of surprise, the howl of his bullet, knew it had gone close to the killer.

'Thought you said the sonuver never had a gun. Den!' the man called with a slight tremor in his voice.

Den – likely Denby Cline, Jesse's other son who ramrodded the Delta C spread the Clines owned in the foothills beyond Skywater.

So, it was going to be like that! Ronan had rolled away behind a low rock and this time at least three guns raked his shelter. He kept his head down, spat grit and closed his eyes to escape more. When he opened them he saw more gunflashes, spread out in a ragged line, a couple on the wall, others at ground level.

His rifle crashed in a hammering volley, the lever working smoothly and slickly. The hammer fell on an empty breech and as he moved on to his side, reaching for fresh shells, a boot crunched on gravel behind him. He whirled, bringing the rifle up, as the dim shape of a man towered above him. The rifle barrel hit somewhere soft, and painful, judging by the sick-sounding grunt.

The man must have crept up during the racket of gunfire and was now writhing on the ground, moaning, hands tight between his legs. Ronan was lunging to his feet when a gun butt crushed in his hat and the world spun away beneath him. He sprawled across his disarrayed bedroll, the rifle clattering from his grip.

His vision was blurred, shot through with darts of light, and he heard rough voices but couldn't make out any words.

The first kick in the ribs told him what to expect, though. . . .

Someone used his pushed-in hat to scoop up some water from the rockpool and fling it into his face. He choked and spluttered and rolled to a half-sitting position. A boot kicked the supporting arm from under him and he sprawled again.

The same boot rested across his throat and he held his breath as he looked past a bent leg clad in dusty and cowpat-spattered denim. Someone had tossed some more sticks on the fire and he saw the big man who belonged to the boot and the stained trousers.

His features were a younger version of Jesse Cline's, which made him almost certainly the other son, Denby. There was a heavy moustache and the eyes either side of the hatchet nose looked just as mean as the elder Cline's.

'Rid all the way in from our south pasture to meet you, Ronan.' The voice was rough maybe from swallowed dust on the long ride, or maybe always that way. 'Handy with your fists they tell me, when you're up agin some kid without any trainin'!'

The boot thudded into Ronan's side again and he grunted, grabbed his ribs as he looked up at his assailant, teeth gritted in pain. 'That "kid" was a mean little bastard – just didn't know any better. Now I've met you and your old man I can see why.'

'Yeah? Well, thanks for the compliment!' Denby kicked him again then jerked his head to two other semi-seen shapes. The men reached down and hauled the gasping Ronan to his feet, slamming him back against the rock wall.

Denby hit him in the midriff and he doubled over but was yanked upright again by the men holding his arms. Denby pulled his sweat-hardened work gloves on more tightly, thrust his face close to Ronan's grimacing features.

'Just kinda evenin' things up, Ronan. You're the pro; me, I'm an amateur. Mind you, amateur *champeen* fighter in this neck of the woods. But I figure softenin' you up a little is allowable, eh, fellers?'

'Sure, Den, sure it is!'

'Go for your life, Den!'

'Kick the crap outta him, way he musta done to Farley!' a man with Indian-like features said viciously.

Denby's face straightened at the words and his eyes seemed to drop a curtain behind them, looked blank and frightening, like a corpse staring out of eternity.

'Yeah! My kid brother, an' you beat him to death.'

'Wanna try to up my "Cline" score by one, Denby?'

Denby Cline was surprised by the slurred words and by the time that split second of inaction had passed, Ronan's left shot out and smashed in Denby's face.

The man howled and reeled away drunkenly, grabbing at his blood-spurting nose. There were five men crowded into the small bend of the campsite and three of them hurriedly reached out to steady the rancher.

Ronan was standing there alone now, fists closed and up in the defensive-but-ready position. He crouched slightly. 'Come on, Cline! Or are you all mouth like your old man and the kid? Farley was long on insults but short on guts.'

The taunting words made Denby throw caution to the wind and he lunged forward, teeth bared, growling curses, fists swinging. Ronan moved his feet in a series of short shuffles, turning this way and that as Denby's fists punched only air. Ronan's fists blurred in two stinging jabs, bringing gasps from Denby as he stumbled drunkenly.

'We grab him, Den?' asked one of the men.

Denby shook his head as his ears rang from the impact of the blows. 'Leave him, for now!'

He caught Ronan off guard as he suddenly jerked a backhand blow that took the prize-fighter on the side of the jaw. Ronan hit the stone wall, jarring his shoulder as some sharp edges of rock cut through his shirt and into his flesh. He staggered right in front of Trace Burdin and the big ramrod was ready, arms swinging in wide, looping blows. The first two knocked Ronan along the wall. He bent over, sagging as the breath was beaten out of him, tried to straighten as Burdin bulled in, lifting a knee towards Ronan's face.

Matt swayed away by pure instinct, felt the rough cloth of the other's trousers scrape his ear in a surge of burning pain. It shot through his system and the old training cut in instinctively. He dodged the next two swings without effort, came up inside Trace's arms and drove his fists like a full-bore jack-hammer into the man's ribs and chest.

Burdin staggered, spun like a top in an effort to stay on his feet, body jerking and shuddering as if on the end of a rope.

Ronan strode after him, protecting his own face, eyes narrowed, against the deceitful flickering of the fire. Trace wasn't set square when a straight right took him in the face, splitting one cheek open beside the mangled, bloody nose.

He twisted away like a drunk trying to avoid an obstacle in his path, groaning as he fought to keep his balance. Then Ronan was beside him, concentrating on his target. He didn't notice Denby coming in from the side until the man hooked him on the jaw, uppercut him hard enough to lift him to his toes, and measured him for the finishing punch.

Then all the Delta C men crowded in and grabbed him, pinning his arms, clouting him across the head, thrusting him back against the wall. They pulled his arms out to the side and Burdin kicked his feet apart so he would be steadier, held in position like a stretched-out living figure 'X'.

'Den! He's all yours! Finish the son of a bitch!'

Denby straightened painfully, face a bloody mess, his work gloves ripped and stained with Ronan's blood, a few small bits of flesh stuck to the leather. He swayed, wiped the back of a glove across his bleeding nostrils, blinking. Then his dark eyes came into focus and fixed on the hard-breathing Ronan.

'Call you "Rip" Ronan, huh?' Denby laughed briefly. 'Good! 'Cause I'm gonna "rip" you to shreds!'

His voice rose in a falsetto as his rage took over and he growled and muttered and snarled like some kind of animal as he bent his head and ploughed in, arms jerking, fists making solid, smacking blows as they punished Ronan's upper body. He rocked and moaned and gritted his teeth, unable to break the grip of the others. He felt weird, almost floating, like the life was beginning to leave him. . . .

By a massive effort he managed to lift one leg and kick Denby in the shins. The man howled like a sick wolf, danced a brief pain-fuelled war dance, then renewed his attack.

Denby could barely stand when he was finished, staggering, supported by the bloody Burdin. He blinked, looked around, sweat jerking from his long hair. 'Where is he?'

'At your feet, Den. That slab of raw meat in front of your boots. You done him over good.'

Denby Cline wiped sweat and blood from his eyes and sniffed and spat before he got Ronan's battered figure into focus. He chuckled, the blood bubbling from his nostrils. Denby spat again, this time into Ronan's face.

The unconscious man didn't stir. 'He still breathin'. . . ?'

42

'Yeah, Den, but reckon he won't take much more.'

'Too bad, 'cause I'm just gettin' started.'

He lifted a boot heel above Ronan's blood-streaked face but the cowboy with the long hair and Indian looks grabbed his arm.

'Whoa, Den! Don't kill him! It'd be murder.'

Denby rounded on the man and punched him hard in the midriff, watching him gag and stumble aside.

'He's right, Den,' Trace Burdin proffered hesitantly. 'Jesse said not to kill him.'

Denby looked murderous but suddenly sobered at mention of his father. Wildly, he looked around, stumbled over one of Ronan's outstretched arms, swearing. Then he stopped and continued to stare at the arm – and the hand with the scarred knuckles at the end of it.

His smashed lips pulled back from his teeth in a bloody smile. He leaned down cautiously, lifted the arm and let it drop so that the limp hand fell across the end of a deadfall log about eight inches in diameter.

He raised swelling eyes to the stiff faces of the men gathered round him.

'Someone get me a – a rock,' he ordered. 'A *big* one.'

CHAPTER 5

SOUTHPAW

First there was the nausea, and, by hell! that was bad enough.

Then the pain. It wiped the sour taste out of his mouth and the throbbing in his head; the throbbing was worse, much worse, elsewhere. Ribs, gut, arms, shoulders felt as if they'd been wrenched out of their sockets, loose teeth, right eye almost closed; the other one gave only blurred vision.

But he didn't need to see: he *felt* and *knew* what he was feeling. That triggered the nausea again and he groaned, keeping his eyes closed. He jumped when he felt a cool, caring hand close gently on his forehead.

'Just sit quietly against the pillows and try to relax.' A glass of cool water touched his lips, felt good. 'Sip slowly.' It was a woman's voice, that sounded like it belonged to one of mature years. He turned his

44

head, got a hazy look at a pleasant middle-aged face, grey-streaked hair tied in a knot behind the head, attentive eyes regarding him.

'The plaster isn't quite set yet. If you move about it may cause it to shift and it won't give proper support.'

He knew he stared and there was a kind of funny feeling about his mouth: sore, brief, splitting pain, a little numbness. He wasn't aware that he had tried to speak.

'I think you're probably asking where you are and what's happened to you,' the woman said in that soothing voice. 'You're in my husband's small infirmary, in Skywater. His name's Doctor Swanston. You've been hurt. Some damage to your ribs, and body, a mild concussion is suspected.'

'H-hand.' The word grated out of a raw throat and even through the blurriness he saw the woman's face straighten. Then she nodded, as if making a decision.

'Yes, I'm afraid your right hand has been very badly . . . damaged. Crushed. The bones are broken but my husband has hopes you'll be able to have restricted use of your fingers – in time.'

Christ! What the hell had happened? Use his fingers again – *in time?* How could he fight if he – *Fight?* No, wait, he had left the tent circuit years ago. Gulbranson said he couldn't use him any more because of what had happened to the kid. . . .

Which kid? He must have spoken aloud because the woman said quietly, 'The young Cline boy. It was all a long time ago. You mustn't worry about it now. Go back to sleep. Doctor will be in shortly and I think Mr Barlow is going to come, too.'

His mind swirled, drifted. *Barlow? Who was that? The 'Cline' boy. . . ?* Wait! Where did all those rocks come from? Small mountains of them, ants crawling over them. *Not ants, fool! Men! Like you, like you!* With hammers, prybars. . . .

It was too much for his pain-filled body and mind to cope with, these crowding visions, and without realizing it, he spun away into oblivion once again.

His teeth chattered with cold behind his battered lips, but his brain felt fevered.

His head was clearer when he woke. A man with lank grey hair spilling across a wrinkled forehead, and who he figured was the doctor, was speaking, but not to him. There was someone else in the room beyond the ambit of his vision.

'Chloroform and laudanum are wearing off now. He'll be more aware of where he is – and of his injuries. You can stay for a short time, but if he shows signs of wanting to sleep again, you must leave at once. Call my wife if I'm not handy.'

'OK, Doc. Anythin' I should tell him? Or *not* tell him?'

'As I said, he'll be aware of his injuries. You know what they are. You know *him*. Tell him what you think he can handle comfortably.'

The doctor left and Ronan tried to focus on his visitor. His vision was clearing slowly, though the right eye didn't seem to be much use to him right now.

'That you, Barlow?'

'Yeah. How you feel, Matt? Agh! Stupid question. You must feel like you've been caught in a stampede.'

'There was one, wasn't there? Not long back. . . ?'

'Few nights ago. You helped stop it, but you weren't injured in that. You were beaten up. By Denby Cline. You recollect him? He had some of his hardcases with him. Seems they caught you in the pass through the mountains.'

Ronan was silent and beneath the bruising and cuts and iodine stains, the trail boss could see the memory returning, watched the split, puffy lips tighten even though they oozed beads of blood, the bruised and swollen jaw firm-up.

He remembered, all right.

'What'd he do to my hand?' His voice was very hoarse.

'Doc said he must've used a rock – pulled a lot of pieces of shale out of the mess. Sorry, didn't mean to. . . .'

By now Ronan was looking down at himself, was surprised to see his torso almost completely encased in plaster up to his armpits. He had been aware of its support but hadn't been alert enough to discover what it was.

His lower right arm was separately encased in thick plaster, his hand covered, and on over the knuckles, halfway down his blackened fingers. His thumb protruded through a special hole, and looked as if a bear

47

had been chewing on it. *Felt like it,* too!

'Jumped me in that pass,' he rasped, the memory stirring again. 'Took a few shots at me to make me keep my head down while Cline and some men got close enough to grab me. Held me while he beat me up. Don't recollect my hand, though.'

'He mangled it real bad.' Barlow was a believer in not mincing words: a man was either tough enough to take the truth or you told him nothing. No lies, no pussy-footing about. Give it to him straight and uncompromising, or not at all.

Ronan nodded, that awful, battered face very grim.

'I guess I didn't walk here?'

'No. I was kinda worried about leavin' you out there. So I rode out from Skywater. Rainin' like hell, still is as you can likely hear.' Barlow smiled crookedly. '*That's* how the damn place got its name by the way, not because of any pretty reflection of blue sky in the lake like we thought! It rains here 'most every week, they tell me. River's still too high to get the cows across. I'll be pushin' to get to Dodge as the first herd of the season and name my own price. Still there's good graze while we're stuck here.'

Ronan wasn't really interested, kept staring at his hand. 'Not ever gonna be much good to me now.'

Barlow shifted uncomfortably. 'Not for prize-fightin' anyway, if that's what you were thinking.'

'How about earnin' a living?'

The trail man shrugged. 'You can adapt, I guess. Use your left hand more, learn to be a southpaw.'

'Hell, that don't always work! I've known men who've tried for one reason or another. Some were good enough, but never as good as with their natural hand.'

'Well, what the hell you expect after someone smashing it up with a rock?' Barlow's voice was harsh, driving. 'Lucky Doc didn't have to cut it off.'

Ronan started, nodded slowly. 'Guess I'm lucky at that. Bein' a prize-fighter, I've had to learn to use my left hand a lot, protecting my jaw, throwin' straight punches, settin' up for my right cross or an upper-cut.' He sighed heavily. 'I guess I'll manage: I'll have to, and not just for roping or that kinda stuff.'

Barlow frowned, watching as Ronan lifted his mostly unscathed left hand, flexed and wriggled his index finger several times, then stiffened it, thumb raised, turned it towards Barlow and bent and straightened the thumb three or four times.

Like a gun hammer falling.

He drifted in and out of disturbed sleep, lying awake during the dark hours, tossing, turning, dreaming of things from his past and other dreams that were nightmarish.

He awoke, sweating, from one of these, found himself gasping and remembered it had been one of those dreams where he had been trying to run from some terror and couldn't move his feet.

'You with us, mister? You hear me?'

Ronan got his breathing under control, rolled his head to see who had spoken, using his reasonably

49

'good' eye. The image was blurred at first, resolved itself to show a raw-boned lanky man about his own age, horse-faced with a thin gingery beard fringing a pointed jaw, a matching moustache above his mean mouth. Light blinked from the sheriff's star pinned to his vest, worn over a faded grey shirt.

'Jack Ifield. Heard you fell off a mountain.'

'Heard wrong.' Ronan's voice was still raspy.

'That so? What's your version?'

Matt Ronan told him haltingly, seeing the scepticism clearly on the long face. The man even began to shake his head.

'Hogwash, friend. The Clines are highly respected folk in this neck of the woods. They don't go beatin' up on saddletramps just for the hell of it. You steal somethin' of theirs, mebbe?'

'Yeah.' The word was unexpected and Ifield blinked. Before he could speak, Ronan continued. 'I stole the life of Farley Cline.'

Ifield's mouth worked silently, sea-green eyes narrowing. 'You're that feller, huh?'

As if the son of a bitch didn't know before coming in here!

'Killed young Farley in a bare-knuckle fight. You shoulda got jail for life. Or a rope.'

'Close the door when you leave, Sheriff. I've got nothing to say to you.'

Ifield's rawboned body tensed and he even dropped his right hand to the butt of his holstered Colt. He looked paler as he drilled those cold eyes into the bed-ridden man.

'Mebbe I've got somethin' to say to you! Like this:

you made a big mistake, killin' that boy, intentional or otherwise. But you'll find out your biggest mistake of all was comin' here into my bailiwick and rilin' my friends.'

'Aaah! Somehow I figured you might be friendly with the Clines. Go away, Sheriff. I'm tired.'

The lawman stood abruptly. 'By Godfrey, no saddlebum is gonna come into my town and speak to me like that.'

'It just happened, Jack,' said Doc Swanston from the doorway. 'I don't know how you snuck in here without us seeing you, but I'm ordering you out – now.'

Ifield looked amused. '*You're* orderin' *me?*'

'That's right. Mr Ronan is my patient and you're upsetting him. If you want to make a legal deal about this, Jack, I'll just send my wife to get Seamus O'Malley and he can make out the papers right here on the spot.'

Ifield was furious but the threat of having a writ or somesuch taken out against him by the toughest and most respected lawyer in the county drained a lot of the anger out of him. But not the resentment at being treated in that way.

He glared at the medic, flicked his gaze to Ronan and said through gritted teeth, 'You get better quick, then leave my town, pronto!'

He shouldered the medic roughly aside and slammed the door after him. Ronan looked a mite drained and the doctor went to his side, and began using his stethoscope after placing a thermometer beneath Ronan's tongue.

'You've got a strong heart, Mr Ronan, and it's beating like a war drum right now.' He squinted at the thermometer without comment and put it away in its case. 'I'll do my best to keep the sheriff away from you until you're in a more fit state to handle him – not that you didn't do very well just now . . . considering.'

'Only one question, Doc – how long?'

Doc Swanston eased himself into the straight-back chair beside Ronan's bed, took out a bent-stem pipe and began to pack it.

'How long will it take you to recover? Man, you are doing ten times better than I expected. But then, being a pugilist in the manner you were earning a living, and, later, spending so much time swinging a sledge hammer on the rockpile, I should not be surprised at your progress. You're fit as a young mountain goat, despite what I've heard is a terrible prison diet, and if you'll pardon the comparison. Something's working in your favour. As your friend Barlow would say, "*You're doin' just fine, pardner.*" ' The medic smiled, a little embarrassed. 'Forgive my poor imitation of your friend.'

'Sounded just like him, Doc. But, *how long*? Days, weeks. . . ?'

'Several weeks to be on the safe side. Now don't look like that. If you wish to be stupid and discharge yourself at an earlier date than I set, then by all means do so, but don't ever show yourself on my doorstep again, no matter how serious or urgent your problem might be because I will not tend you.'

'Kind of bossy, ain't you?'

'Take it or leave it, my friend. I spent years studying to be a doctor and I like to think I can judge when a patient is recovering sufficiently to leave my care. If they wish to dispute my decision, then they should not have bothered to come to me in the first place.'

Ronan frowned. His face was still blotchy with fading bruises and healing scrapes and cuts. He had less pain but his muscles and body were still mighty sore when he moved, which was not as often as he would have liked. He had had a practical demonstration once or twice of the doctor's wisdom when he tried to get out of bed, or made other movements at that time forbidden by the crusty old sawbones.

'All right, Doc. I'm just impatient, but I know I'm not in very good shape to do much more than roll a cigarette – and I even make a mess of that, one-handed.'

'You'll eventually master it – as you will whatever else you want to do – except, of course, you won't be able to return to prize-fighting – or gun-fighting, if that was one of your interests.' He saw Ronan's eyes cloud and added, 'Using your right hand, that is. Of course, you can work at more or less mastering your left. It is difficult but it can be done.'

'Reckon I'll be able to handle a rifle, Doc?'

'You may manage, but you will not necessarily get consistent accuracy. I'm afraid the nerves in your hand are irreparably damaged and will be prone to random actions, sudden or cramping, beyond your conscious control.'

Ronan's face was grey now beneath the bruises. 'Nothin' like giving it straight from the shoulder eh, Doc?'

'I had you down as a man who would prefer that, Mr Ronan.'

Ronan nodded gently. 'Yeah, just don't like to hear confirmed what I've been worrying about, I guess.'

'Understandable.' The medic stood slowly, took another puff on his pipe. 'If I can offer just one piece of advice – you'd be wise to forget about squaring things with Denby Cline.' He gave a slight shake of his head. 'Well, after Jack Ifield's visit, I'm sure you realize you are up against tremendous odds, Mr Ronan. Tremendous.'

As the doctor left the room, Ronan gently massaged his right forearm, rubbing a thumb lightly over the plaster covering the back of his hand, back and forth, back and forth. . . .

Hell, he was used to going against the odds.

'Story of my life, Doc!' he called as Swanston closed the door after him.

CHAPTER 6

DODGE CITY BLUES

When the river finally dropped enough for the herd to be pushed across – even though it was supper time and the sun was sinking fast behind the range – Barlow decided to make his move.

'Drop your grub and grab your gear,' Barlow bawled. 'We're goin' across before this damn country decides to start rainin' on us again.'

There were plenty of curses and moans and groans but Barlow was a decent trail boss mostly and didn't make many hard demands so the men obeyed quickly enough. In a matter of minutes, only Mr McRostie was left to do all the swearing himself as he extinguished the cookfires, rinsed the utensils and threw them crankily into the restored chuckwagon.

He had to admit it was handling better with the repaired axle and new spokes in the broken front wheel, but he hated river crossings.

None of the men liked the chore very much, working in the near-dark; the half-moon had grown into a full orb but it was not yet risen completely and the light was uncertain enough for cowboys to miss seeing stragglers.

So much so that by the time the dripping, bawling, edgy cows stumbled up the far bank they found that ten had been swept away. That was more money than Barlow wanted to lose but it was one of the risks he had taken when he had chosen to listen to that old panhandling prospector who had told him about this alternative trail to Dodge City.

If he followed directions and there was no more rain, his herd would be the first of the season and therefore able to command the highest prices for a beef-starved town.

They had successfully crossed the Skywater and now had to drive forty miles to the Arkansas, a much bigger and faster-flowing river, before they would be able to reach Dodge City.

Though this was said to be Indian country, they didn't see a single warrior, though a few smoke columns in the distance told Barlow they were under observation.

But they made the Arkansas and Spurs, scouting ahead, found a place where there were sandbanks and alternate shallows and channels where he figured they could cross.

It was the best place, but it was a hell of a lot of hard work to keep the bawling steers away from the deeper water. By the time the whole herd was across and heading for grassland at a jog-trot, they had lost another dozen head.

Barlow was annoyed, but deep down knew he could likely afford the loss as long as his herd was still the first into Dodge – then he could name his own price. . . .

When three riders came out of the trees, two in range clothes and one in a frock coat and broadcloth trousers, wearing a Derby hat, he instinctively drew his Winchester from the saddle scabbard. Several of his crew did the same and the trio stopped a hundred feet away, Derby Hat lifting a hand, palm out.

'Easy, *amigos*!' He grinned, an amiable man, lightly bearded and with long hair protruding from under the small hat. 'I am speaking to the Texas herd from Wilbur County, pride of the Lone Star State, am I not?'

'You are . . . whoever you are.'

'Ah, yes, a genuine Texan, I see! Sir, I am Hugh McGill, the top cattle agent in Dodge City and, if I may say so, somewhat blushingly, probably the top meat man anywhere.'

'I've heard of you, Mr McGill. I'm Skip Barlow and this is my herd and for sale. Am I first?'

McGill laughed aloud, grinned at the two sober men with him. 'First? I should smile you are! No one has used this trail in ten years, even though the Indians have been more or less "tamed" for that long. Yes, sir, you are first into Dodge this season and I'm here to pay you top price for two thousand head,

I estimate, roughly. . . .'

'Give or take a couple of dozen. Your rivers ain't all that friendly.'

'Well, I'll try and make up for their shortcomings! Let's say two thousand head and we can get an exact count later. Have you a price in mind?'

'I have. Thirty-five dollars a head.'

McGill reeled slightly, but nodded: *This lazy-looking Texan knew the market, damn it*! 'That sounds a little high but a firm price, sir?'

'Firm like that big boulder over your left shoulder. Be mighty hard to move.'

'Then I agree to pay thirty-five dollars per head with the proviso that your cows are not carrying that dreaded tick fever your state is unfortunately – er – infamous for.'

'You won't find tick fever in any herd I bring to market, mister,' Barlow said curtly, clearly offended at the suggestion.

McGill lifted his hand again, palm out. 'I have to ask, sir. You must understand that.'

'Yeah, I guess. OK.' Barlow rode forward and thrust out his right hand. 'You want to shake on thirty-five and guaranteed no tick fever?'

'I do, and with pleasure, Mr Barlow. I have waited a long time to meet you. Your first time making market at Dodge, I believe?'

'Yeah. I've tried Abilene and Hays City, Ellsworth and Wichita. Steered clear of Dodge, because of its reputation as a hell town, but you seem to have a good grip on law and order there right now.'

'Ah, yes. Our famous Marshal Earp enforces the Town Ordinance with a firm hand. Shall we ride in and seal the deal at our brand new First National Bank of Kansas?'

The two range-clad men with McGill stayed with the herd and Barlow rode alongside McGill on the trail to town. Up close he could see that the agent had that indefinable steely look to his somewhat small eyes – something he had noticed in many cattle agents and other hucksters who could talk smoothly while they sold you something that would make them a profit. It was to be expected.

Barlow looked behind several times and saw the dust cloud from the herd lifting, on the move and in the right direction. 'You are uneasy, sir?'

'No, I reckon I can get my gun out faster than you.'

McGill's seemingly permanent smile tightened. 'I am not sure I care for that remark, Mr Barlow!'

'Don't let it bother you. It's just an old Texas way of saying I reckon I can take care of myself.'

McGill stared back then laughed shortly. 'I believe you, sir! Well, let's speed things up a little and we'll be in Dodge in time to have a few drinks before supper, with all the contracts signed. All right?'

'Lead the way.'

But when they came to the new red-brick building with the freshly painted sign above the double glass doors proclaiming it to be the *First National Bank Of Kansas, Assets $750,000*, the reception that awaited them was both unexpected – and damned danger-ous.

The gunshots inside the bank sounded flat, like someone hammering nails in a house next door, and then the upper panels of the right-hand front door shattered and splinters flew. Folk on the boardwalks yelled and screamed – according to gender – and hunted cover, running this way and that, some into the street, others down the narrow alley beside the bank, a couple crouching behind sidewalk rainbutts.

Then the doors were kicked open so hard one was wrenched off its hinges and five men wearing ban-dannas over their lower faces came out, all holding smoking guns, two carrying canvas sacks that sagged – and not with the weight of groceries.

Barlow wrenched his horse around, dragging out his Colt instinctively. McGill had gone pale and spurred away back across the street, leaning forward, raking with his spurs, horse stretching out, getting out of range.

He had virtually abandoned Barlow who hardly noticed as the bank robbers ran for the alley. He heard a woman scream down there and a man yell, followed by two rapid gunshots. The bunch ran hard into the alley as the getaway horses were driven out by another masked man, holding a smoking six-gun.

As the robbers mounted, shooting at Barlow and anyone else who wasn't yet under cover, the trail boss spurred his mount on to the boardwalk and into the doorway of a saddler's shop. The animal whinnied and pranced and kicked, splintering the door, but

Barlow snapped a couple of shots at the robbers, saw one man lurch in the saddle.

One of his companions steadied him and another took three fast shots at Barlow. He reeled as lead burned across his left shoulder; he hit his head on the low door jamb and tumbled from the saddle. His mount leapt across the walk and out into the street where the bandits were now making their escape. The wounded man finally tumbled from his saddle to fall under the pounding hoofs of the horses behind.

The others didn't even look back and his body was sent rolling and skidding through the dust. Some townsmen were belatedly shooting and one man went down under the return fire of the escaping bank robbers. The others ducked for cover.

Then a man suddenly ran out of a narrow doorway with a sign that Barlow learned later read *Marshal's Office*. He held a long-barrelled gun, rifle or shotgun, Barlow couldn't tell right away, and fearlessly stepped into the path of the fleeing robbers. The weapon rose to his shoulder and Barlow saw it was a shotgun now – *a single-barrelled* shotgun! That lawman must be crazy, facing these escaping men with a single shot weapon, men who had already demonstrated their readiness to kill. . . .

Then he watched in disbelief as the marshal began shooting. His first shot took the leader down, hurling him clear of the saddle so hard he actually somersaulted before hitting the ground. *Then*, to Barlow's surprise, the lawman moved his hand swiftly like a striking snake under the barrel, a blurred forward-

and-back movement, and the gun thundered again, blew another robber out of the saddle. The others were veering away now, shooting wildly or not at all, as another of their number fell violently, to lay unmoving in the dust.

The shotgun thundered a third time after another snake-swift movement of the lawman's hand beneath the barrel. It was the outlaw's horse that was hit this time. The robber was thrown hard, hit the dust and lay there dazed, as the shotgun roared once more and the last bank robber threw his gun away and stood in the stirrups, clearly surrendering.

He was too late: a charge of buckshot shredded his right arm, left it dangling by a piece of bloody flesh, and the man collapsed, briefly lost in the heavy pall of swirling gunsmoke. *Judas Priest! Five shots, five downed men!*

Barlow's ears were ringing with the echoing thunder of that truly deadly weapon. He still couldn't believe his eyes: a single-barrelled shotgun that fired five times!

Doc Swanston considered Ronan's recovery was swift and unusual, but Matt himself didn't think so.

Hell, he didn't even like to count the years he had been on the wrong end of calloused fists and worse – sometimes the local lads managed to conceal a roll of dimes or quarters or a short piece of lead in their hands and a blow with that much weight added could knock a horse off its feet. He had caught them a couple of times, once ending up with a broken jaw and a long lay-off before Gulbranson would take him back as one of his team.

In those rough towns, when he would go to the stores or, more usually, for a glass of beer on a hot day, someone always seemed to recognize him from the platform outside the fight tent. Then there would be barroom challenges that couldn't be accepted and, at the same time, damn well couldn't be ignored, either. Sometimes Gulbranson would be able to head off trouble by buying a few rounds of drinks; other times the fight had to happen and nobody was a winner, and surely not Ronan.

There had been other times when he had been jumped in dark alleys or the backs of liveries by men who had picked him in the ring and been beaten; they had a lot more courage with three or four of their local pards swinging alongside them.

He had been stomped by horses, shot in the back – twice – and, once, a scalp-crease that put him in a coma for a week. But he had recovered from everything and, add to that the really rough treatment in prison, and it was little wonder that he considered his beating at the hands of Denby Cline not much worse than anything he had experienced over the years. Except that this time his right hand was crippled.

But, get knocked down, get right back up – he knew no other way.

The doctor examined the hand closely the day he removed the plaster and while Ronan was in pretty fair shape in general, Swanston tightened his lips and looked him straight in the eye.

'It's worse than I thought, son, I'm sorry.' No comment. 'Look for yourself. See the way those fingers are kind of clawed. . . ?'

'Seem about right to get a good grip on the edge of a saloon bar,' Ronan quipped, but his stomach was knotted as he studied the blackened and lacerated hooked fingers: he knew what the sawbones was going to say.

'I thought we might try some intense therapy on your fingers, try to straighten them and get you almost half the original movement back, but—'

Ronan stiffened. 'They ain't gonna stay clawed like that, are they?'

'I wouldn't care to say right out "no", in fact, I certainly wouldn't even say "maybe", not just now.'

'There a little hope in there somewhere, Doc?'

'Not much. You prefer that I'm honest with you and don't beat about the bush, I take it?'

'Give it to me straight, Doc. I can handle it.'

'All right. I *believe* the hand will stay partially clawed, at least for some time. I'll still attempt therapy but it will be hard, time-consuming and definitely painful.'

'Sounds familiar.'

Swanston looked at him sharply: the man wasn't boasting or even making a feeble joke; he was merely commenting and Swanston knew this was one tough *hombre* who had been through more pain that most men would experience in two lifetimes, but was still ready and willing to stand up to it – and fight it off as best he could.

'Then we'll begin in the morning. I'll leave the plaster off now, but I'll bind your hand firmly and, I think, each finger separately.' At Ronan's puzzled look, he added, 'They vary in their injuries and each one needs a different pressure. Your thumb is mostly lacerated so I think you'll regain almost total movement there.'

Ronan stared at the medic and then winked by way of comment. Swanston shook his head slowly.

'You'll need to be tough about this, Mr Ronan. I wouldn't want you to think otherwise. The bones are too damaged to knit in any kind of useful alignment, so, unfortunately, that means a lot of pain, and no guarantee of real success.'

'You do what you have to, Doc – give it your best.'

The doctor sighed, stood up, pushing his hands against his thighs for leverage. He looked mighty weary, was always being called out to someone who needed him.

Right now was one of those times it seemed.

'Have a lady worried about her pregnancy. It's a long ride, so I think I'll fortify myself against the possibility of rain with some of this bourbon. I believe a small dose or two might help you sleep, Mr Ronan?'

'You're a pretty good sawbones, Doc. I feel exactly the same way.'

CHAPTER 7

NO GUNS IN TOWN

It wasn't good enough! He simply couldn't get the hang of handling a six-gun with his left hand. It just didn't feel right, somehow. He chuckled bitterly at his thought – *left – right – right – left. . . .*

Made no difference: his hand wasn't used to the weight of the gun and he had already found out that wearing the right-hand holster on his left hip with the gun butt pointing forward took the efforts of a contortionist to get it free of leather without the risk of blowing his foot off.

He was using the far corner of Doc Swanston's land: the infirmary and Swanston's house were a hundred-plus yards away at the end of a side street. But the town was not far beyond and when he finally gave up on perfecting a fast draw – *perfecting? Hell, he'd be happy if he could get the Colt out just once without fumbling and dropping the damn thing!* – he decided he would try shooting at a target.

A handful of bottles and empty jam jars from Doc's trash pit gave him what he needed and he lined up half-a-dozen of varying sizes on top of the rear fence rail. There was only brush and trees beyond. Then he lifted the Colt, went through a short period of pain as he forced his left wrist into the clawed fingers on his right hand, aiming to steady the Colt ... if only he could get any kind of a grip.

Sweat broke out on his forehead. His shoulder and arm ached as he tried to lift it in co-ordination with the other hand and the six-gun. When he fired there was a ramming sensation all the way up into his right shoulder and he bit back a curse.

To his surprise, when the gunsmoke cleared, he saw one of the preserve jars had been shattered. *But what an effort!* If he had to go through that every time, he might just as well walk unarmed into an argument that had deteriorated into gunplay, because a 5-year-old child could get a gun working faster than he had.

But – *he had hit a target*! So he had to try again, endure the pain and discomfort long enough to sight and fire.

His hand wasn't steady enough but he decided to be charitable with himself and believe that *in time* not only would his accuracy improve, but his shooting speed, too.

Who d'you think you're kidding? This was suicide stuff. And he couldn't see any way out, except endless, painful practice, which was by no means certain to succeed.

He only hit two jars out of six, but it was better than total misses. He persevered and was reloading for the fifth time when a voice said sharply, 'Stop right there, mister! Who gave you permission to shoot off a gun in this town?'

It was Jack Ifield, of course, his stringy moustache bristling as his long, thin legs brought him up the slope, right hand resting on the butt of his holstered six-gun.

'It's agin the Ordinance to shoot here.'

The unaccustomed exertions made Ronan's breathing come hard and he staggered a little as he turned quickly to face the lawman, his half-loaded revolver down at his side. His right wrist and forearm were still in a plaster cast, his crooked fingers splayed a little and were awkward with separate bandages on each one, the whole supported by a narrow sling: his whole right side *hurt*!

'Guess I never thought about it, Sheriff,' he said, gaspingly. He looked pale and the fading bruises and cuts stood out against the pallor. He had lost several pounds and his clothes hung on him loosely: he looked like a saddlebum, and knew it. 'Bored crazy in that infirmary. Just figured I'd see if I could handle a gun left-handed.'

The lawman's pale eyes narrowed. 'You got some notion of goin' after Denby Cline?'

'I figure if we meet up sometime, might be as well for me to know if I can shoot a gun with my left hand.'

Ifield shook his head. 'No, Ronan. Not in my town

68

– or my county. Ignorance of the Town Ordinance don't count with me, but, seein' as you've been laid up and sufferin' for, what? Goin' on a month now? Near enough, I might just overlook this. But you hand over your guns and I'll keep 'em till you leave.'

Ronan had his breathing under better control now. 'I don't care to do that, Sheriff.'

'Know somethin'? I just don't *care*! Period! I'm law in this town and that's my decision. Besides,' suddenly his pistol was in in his right hand, covering Ronan, the hammer cocked. He grinned crookedly. 'There's this.'

Ronan couldn't push it. He holstered the Colt then fumbled and strained with his left hand to reach the belt buckle of the rig while Ifield watched, not offering any help. Ronan tossed the belt and holster at the lawman's feet. Jack Ifield thrust out his jaw.

'You hand that to me proper!'

Ronan dropped on to a log where he had propped the Winchester and shook his head. 'I'm pooped.'

'Then slide away from that rifle!'

Ronan sighed and obeyed, sweat running into his eyes now. He felt light-headed and tight in the chest. His busted hand throbbed! He had to admit his efforts to use it to support the guns were not successful.

Ifield watched him closely as he scooped up the gunbelt, hooking it over his left shoulder, then lifted the rifle by the muzzle. He looked more relaxed when he had possession of the weapons. 'When you leavin'?'

Ronan shrugged, his healing ribs giving him a stab that made him wince. 'Pretty soon, I guess. Doc can't do much more for me. That son of a bitch Denby crippled me good.'

'Hell, you killed his brother! Anyway, was a fair fight was what I was told.' Ronan snorted and spat at that. 'Just your bad luck the damage turned out to be so permanent.'

'Bad luck for someone.' Ronan stood slowly, still not feeling all that steady on his feet.

'Where the hell you think you're goin'?' Ronan kept walking slowly down the slope towards the distant house. Guns under one arm, Ifield came after him, reaching to grab his left arm, almost pulling Ronan off-balance. 'I'm talkin' to you!'

'You can do it without manhandling my patient, Jack!' Doc Swanston had appeared on the back porch of his house, still wearing his hat and riding clothes from the visit that had taken him out of town a few hours earlier. Now he puffed up the slope and stood beside Ronan, looking at him critically. 'You shouldn't've left the house.'

'Needed a change of air, Doc. But don't get yourself in Dutch with this sonuver on my account.'

'Hey! You watch your mouth!'

Swanston held Ronan's arm and guided him towards the porch steps. 'For God's sake get that blasted chip off your shoulder, Jack! The whole damn town's tired of it. Go back to your office and write yourself up a report.'

Ifield coloured but didn't reply, watched tight-lipped as Swanston led Ronan into the house. Then he strode away, flinging the guns on to the porch as he did so.

Sitting at the kitchen table, whiskey-laced coffee in a china mug before him, the grey-faced Ronan looked across at Swanston.

'Doc, you know I'm mighty grateful for all you've done, but I reckon I'd better move on. Ifield's gonna be a pain in the butt and, well, these walls seem to be getting closer to my bed every time I look up, and the air's getting thicker. You know what I mean?'

'Of course. You've been here a long time and you're starting to improve some, and you feel the need to be a little more independent. I understand your desire to try to master shooting your guns with your left hand, but you have to realize it will take time – a lot of time. You're not a natural southpaw, and although you have some advantage in how you've used your left hand in your fights, it still won't be easy, with six-gun or rifle.'

He waited but Ronan said nothing.

'I'm sure you believe you need to do this – and I can only think you have some kind of vengeance in mind.'

'Let's just say that Denby Cline might be a lot better off if he doesn't cross my trail.'

'Perhaps that applies to you, too – if you don't cross his.'

Ronan shrugged. 'Our trails'll cross, Doc. I'll make sure of that.'

Swanston heaved a sigh and nodded. 'Yes, I can

see it's inevitable. Well, it so happens that I know of a place that might suit you for practicing with your guns, a few miles out of town and up into the ranges a little way; unfortunately, not all that far from the Delta C spread, which, I'm sure you know, is owned by the Cline family.'

'Hey, Doc, I don't want you to get into any trouble with them Clines by helping me.'

Swanston lifted his hand. 'I'm thinking of someone else, the, er, tenant of the land I'm referring to.' He paused and studied Ronan's puzzled face. 'How do you feel about Indians?'

Ronan's frowned deepened. 'I take 'em as I find 'em, same as I do white men, or black or any other colour.'

'I'm very glad to hear it, because this person has some Indian blood – Cheyenne, I believe.'

Ronan waited, nodding slightly. 'Don't matter to me. What is he, a half-breed? Quarter-breed. . . ?'

'We-ell, you see, to start with, it's not a "he".'

Ronan blinked and then half-rose out of his chair.

Doc Swanston smiled. 'She's quite young, and rather good looking. Here! You'd better sit down again before you fall down, Mr Ronan.'

Over another cup of coffee, laced a lot more strongly than previously, Doc Swanston told him about the land and the half-breed Indian woman named Water-Lily who now lived on it.

'She's added "Marks" to her name; after the father of her child, which won't be born for six months yet.'

72

'Isn't he going to marry her?'

'He would if he could – but he's dead.' Swanston's voice hardened. 'An accident, they say.'

Ronan glanced at him sharply. 'You don't sound convinced.'

'Oh, there's no way to prove different. He and his horse were found at the foot of a cliff. According to Jack Ifield's findings, an accident. And Trace Burdin, Delta C's foreman, just happened to see it all from a high trail on Cline land which borders that area; claims the horse spooked at something on the cliff edge, possibly a snake. He's the only witness.'

'There's some reason why things would be . . . better for someone if Marks was dead?'

Swanston nodded, face grim. 'Rawley Marks proved up on that section. It was to be his home, with Lily. Jesse Cline figured when Rawley was killed the land would be up for grabs again, but Rawley was smarter than Jesse allowed and had had our top legal man, Seamus O'Malley, draw up his will. He left the land to Lily, who is not yet twenty-one, by the way, so Rawley arranged for me to hold it for her in trust.'

Ronan frowned. 'I'm not well up on such things, but can an Indian inherit land that way?'

'Part Indian – O'Malley says yes, and he's the last man I'd argue with where any kind of law is concerned. I've moved Lily in now I've confirmed her pregnancy. Some of her tribe have been keeping an eye on her but now the government in its wisdom has seen fit to move the Reservation down river, closer to Fort Dodge, they won't be able to do that. It's now

Jack Ifield's duty to see she's not hassled.'

'It'd be Jesse Cline who'd be doing any hassling?'

'Of course. It's good land and Jesse sure doesn't need it, but he's already complaining about having a 'breed for a neighbour. He's not partial to Indians.'

'He'd have plenty of company in this part of the country.'

'Well, he has his reasons. More than twenty years ago his wife was taken hostage by a Cheyenne war party. He eventually got her back but she had been badly treated – *violated* was a word he used a lot. He led a puntive expedition and it was bloody. When he returned he shipped his wife back east and divorced her: damaged goods, in his view. He's never spoken of her since, they say.'

'Maybe I should've fought Jesse instead of Farley.'

Doc half-smiled. 'Yes, not too likeable, is Jesse Cline, and if he can push Lily off, he will. But if you were to go up there to stay – there's a lean-to at the rear of the main cabin – you could practice with your guns and I don't believe Delta C would make any trouble. I'll visit from time to time to see how you're recovering.'

'Doc, I'd do it, but. . . .' Ronan indicated his crippled hand and then his left hand. 'I can't see my being there will keep the likes of Denby Cline or this Burdin away.'

'You might be surprised. You shot two of those jars with that Colt left-handed. Men are much bigger than jars, Matt.'

'I'm slow as a fly in treacle, Doc!'

'Perhaps. Look, Lily is a good woman. She's not

74

immoral despite the way it looks. She and Rawley Marks were genuinely in love. Things happened before the preacher could be called in, which they have a habit of doing, no matter the colour of anyone's skin. Then Marks was killed and she'll probably have to raise the child herself. She's had a pretty rough time as it is, Matt, half-breed, good-looking woman, alone in a country of men – you know what I mean.'

'I dunno how long I could stay, Doc.'

The medic nodded. 'I'd like you to stay on until she comes of age and the land is legally hers.'

'Doc, I owe you so much now for all the treatment, and livin' in your house. . . !'

'Stay and watch out for Lily and we'll be all squared away.'

'I'm not used to bein' obligated to folks.'

'You won't be. I'll be paying you to do a job for me. Is it settled?'

Ronan knew he would not get a better offer and he needed such a breathing space to see just what he was going to be able to do – or not do – with his disability.

He felt uneasy about the chore, out of his depth already – but in the end he agreed.

Swanston was pleased and this time they sealed the deal by drinking the whiskey – without the coffee.

'I'll give you some exercises for your hand and fingers. I want you to do them at least twice a day. Don't expect anything like your original mobility, but you may find your gun prowess improving.'

'I've got an idea it'd better, Doc!'

CHAPTER 8

LONELY LAND

Muttering, Jesse Cline signed the delivery slip for the wagonload of spoke-and-rim timber, flung it at the driver, and stormed back to his office.

He found Denby sitting at his ease, a full glass of Jesse's best brandy in his hand. Denby raised the glass as his father entered and the slight blur edging his words told Jesse this was not the first glass his son had consumed.

'Ah! Welcome, Father! I have been awaiting your presence.'

Jesse, annoyed because the shipment of timber had cost half as much again as usual, *and* was a day late being delivered, stepped around his desk, leaned across and knocked the glass from the startled Denby's hand. The younger Cline brushed at the splashes on his new shirtfront and stood up quickly, swearing.

'The hell'd you do that for?'

'You don't help yourself to *anything* of mine unless I tell you to! You ought to know that. Now get two more glasses and pour us each a shot – yours much smaller than mine.'

Denby's hand shook as he obeyed, the neck of the crystal decanter clinking against the glass rim.

'I'm sorry, Pa. It's just that we brung in that big herd from the mesa and managed to drag in thirty or more of Shack Butler's cows along the way. He can bitch all he wants, but he knows if we look close we'll find he's running-ironed our brand into his on at least half of 'em. I figured it was time he was taught a lesson an' I was just havin' a quiet celebration waiting for you.'

Jesse grunted, drank deeply. 'Well, when he does gripe – and he will – you send Trace over to straighten him out, but good.'

'That's what I aimed to do, Pa. Er, you had some bad news or somethin'?'

Jesse glared. 'Aah, damn price of timber's gone through the roof since those floods. But never mind that. I've heard that Ronan sonuver has moved in with the Indian bitch.' Denby straightened, his mouth agape. 'Swanston apparently sent him up there.'

Denby spluttered. 'Sent *Ronan* up there? What, to protect that damn squaw?'

'It would seem so.' Jesse's eyes were hard. 'You obviously haven't talked to Ifield lately. Ronan's been practising with his guns – using his left hand.'

Denby snorted. 'He'd do better usin' his pecker.'

'According to Ifield, Ronan's getting pretty good now at shooting left-handed.'

Denby frowned. 'He might shoot straighter but, hell, Pa. What good's that do him if it takes him half a day to load and line up on his target? He's nothin' to worry about.'

Jesse's jaw muscles worked and his fist clutching his glass showed white at the knuckles. 'You think that's all there is to it, huh?' He leaned forward so suddenly that Denby reared back in his chair. 'I'm not having any breed within spitting-distance of Delta! She oughta be on the Reservation with the other red bastards.' He almost choked as he uttered the word: it was nowhere near mean enough or insulting enough for Jesse's liking. Denby pursed his lips, let out a long, hissing breath.

He felt his stomach knot as the old hatred he thought his father had learned to live with after all these years showed clear and bitterly on Jesse's taut face, stronger than ever.

'Get that drifter out of there,' Jesse said surprisingly calmly. 'I want her there alone, and I want that cabin shot up every damn week! I *don't* want her harmed, just scared.' He allowed himself a crooked smile, shook his head. 'I was about to say "scared *white*" – not quite fitting, but you get the idea. She'll either sell to me, or she'll quit and go after her lice-ridden kin at the new Reservation. Now. You think you can handle that? You and Trace? Anything else you need, you just let me know, but *get it done*!'

78

'It'll be a pleasure, Pa, a real, gen-u-ine pleasure to lock horns again with that saddlebum.'

Lily, as she preferred to be called, was good looking in an Indian way: that was the best Ronan could come up with when he thought about how he would describe her if asked.

Her Cheyenne blood was obvious enough, the smooth golden skin tones, the flattened eye sockets above the cheekbones, the nose showing a slight bend that would probably become more noticeable as she grew older. Teeth were white, framed by red lips, neither thin nor prominent, and there was no mistaking the touch of iron in the set of her jaw.

Her hair was jet black, of course, braided in the way of her ancestors, forming a frame for the rather broad face that he had seen touched by sundown glow. Ronan had felt a strange *suspended* kind of feeling in his chest; very briefly and nothing he could explain, but that glow had lent her some special kind of beauty that had surprised him. Kind of primitive, maybe.

Her eyes glinted like deep, dark rock pools in the mountains. Under the loose buckskin dress she appeared to be quite slim and probably wiry. The dress itself was beaded around the neckline and there were a few animal bone talismans on a leather thong around her slim neck. Her mother had been the tribal medicine woman and Lily had been taught some of the traditional healings and blessings.

He looked up from oiling the cylinder of his Colt

when she shifted the lantern across the deal table so he could see better, and gave her a slight smile, nodding his thanks.

'You afraid of me, Ro-nan?' she asked abruptly, in that slightly husky voice, startling him. There was a touch of amusement in her face.

He looked up sharply. 'Hell, no! But I might be a mite leery. Not of you, but, well, I've never been responsible for a pregnant woman before.'

She laughed and he momentarily thought of cool mountain water trickling over shining pebbles.

'You funny, Ro-nan! Marks was like that.' The dark, liquid eyes closed in on a memory. 'You think I bad? A whore?'

' 'Cause you took a white man to bed? Nah, I learned early on what's natural in life, even if it don't please some folk to see it that way.'

She studied him as he wiped off the gun and began to push cartridges into the cylinder. 'You like Marks.'

He snapped his head up. 'I'd *like* him? I thought he was dead?'

'No! You *like* him. You . . . same.'

'You mean "white"? Well, can't help that, I guess.'

'*No*! You good like him.'

He smiled crookedly. 'There's plenty would give you an argument about that! But thanks anyway.'

The gun reloaded he slid it into the holster which he wore on his right hip now, reversed, gun butt facing forward. It was a left-hand rig, forgotten by some previous patient at the infirmary. Doc had suggested Ronan use it, set it for a cross-draw, and it worked. He could whip his left hand across his body and snatch that Colt out, cocking the hammer, in the blink of an eye. Only thing was, he dropped it about three times out of ten. But he was working on doing it more smoothly.

He stood now. 'Reckon I'll turn in, Lily. I'm gettin' used to early nights.' He picked up the lantern nearest him by the wire handle, hooking it conveniently over his clawed fingers, and moved towards the door, the lean-to he was using was only a few yards away.

'You want rifle?' She gestured to the Winchester leaning against the wall.

Soberly, he shook his head. 'You keep it here. We'll try it tomorrow. *Buenas noches.*'

She stared at the door after he had closed it behind him, picked up the rifle and laid it on the table. She sat down, hand resting on the oiled blue-metal action.

'I am lucky woman – I meet *three* good white men. First, Rawley Marks, then Doc Swanston – and now Ro-nan.'

She touched her slightly swollen belly. 'I hope you lucky, too.'

She blew out the lantern and sat on, in the dark of the cabin, thinking.

The first bullet tore through the light shingles of the lean-to, shattering three that erupted in stinging splinters before Ronan could roll out of the bunk.

He twisted desperately so he didn't land on his right side, sprawled on the hard-packed earth of the floor, blinking, trying to catch up with his instinctive movments.

A half-dozen other slugs sieved the slanting roof so that stars shone through the gaps.

He had his six-gun in his left hand now, duck-walking on his knees to the flimsy door. It rattled in its frame before he reached it and splinters flew as flattened lead snarled in the dark, confined quarters. He dived full-length on the floor, rolling to the side, out of line with the door. He landed on his right arm and immmediately grunted aloud in pain as it streaked through his elbow and still tender ribs. But he spun his body awkwardly, kicking the sagging door, and it fell outwards with a clatter.

He heard running horses, glimpsed dark shapes tearing across the yard, smearing the stars behind them, then fired two reasonably fast shots. He didn't hit anything, except maybe the spreading cotton-wood up the slope from his shelter.

Then the horsemen raced on and rifles hammered and he heard the lead thunking into the cabin's thick doors and window shutters. Someone gave a wild war cry and for a brief moment he thought '*Indians*?', then heard the drunken words of one of the raiders:

'Shoulda brought a shotgun, Den!'

Denby Cline! Had to be. And one of his Delta C hardcases. Biting back another wave of pain he rose to his knees, leaned against the door frame and raised the six-gun, steadying his arm as well as he could with his clawed fingers on his right hand.

Before he fired there was the whiplashing of a rifle from a window, three – no *four*! – rapid shots. One of the riders yelled and his horse whinnied and lurched sideways in an abrupt movement that tipped the man violently from the saddle. The body spun and skidded across the ground, bringing up in a small cloud of dust outside the lean-to.

Ronan was on his feet in a flash, kicking the last of the damaged door aside as he lunged forward and drove a boot against the man's head. The dazed rider's hat rolled away and in the wan moon and starlight, Ronan saw it was Denby Cline himself – now moaning, semi-conscious.

The rifle hammered again and the second rider yanked violently on his reins, the horse's forelegs stiff, skidding. The man was thrown violently forward, hitting his face against the arched neck of the animal. While he was still dazed, Ronan jumped forward, clipped him with his six-gun and hauled him roughly out of the saddle, The man grunted as he fell and lay at Ronan's feet. Ronan placed a boot across his neck and called:

'Save your ammo, Lily! There's only two of the fools. Bring a lantern.'

She carried the lantern in one hand, the rifle in the other. He noticed she held it with her thumb holding back the hammer, the barrel swinging in the direction of the downed men.

They both sat up, dazed, about the same time. The

yellow light from the storm lantern identified them as Denby Cline and Trace Burdin – Ronan recognized him as one of the men who had held him while Denby beat him unconscious before taking a rock to his gun hand.

She covered them with the rifle while he disarmed them, Burdin's horse standing panting and wide-eyed near the corrals. Denby's mount was unmoving and he saw the glint of blood just under its ear where the girl had shot it.

'Here I was thinking I'd give you some lessons in shooting that Winchester.'

Her teeth flashed briefly. 'Rawley teach me.'

'Did a good job. Now, you fellers with us?' The Delta C men were sitting up, blinking, holding their heads, eyes lifting now to watch Ronan and the girl. 'OK, I smell whiskey. On your way back from a wingding in town, huh?'

Neither answered and he could sense their tension, wondering what was going to happen to them.

Ronan stood over Trace and ordered him to stand. The man did so, slowly, warily, his flabby belly showing white through a gap in his shirt front. Ronan walked around the big man, smelling his sweat mixed with the booze from the Skywater saloon.

'I've heard you like to beat up people, Burdin – men or women; someone even said you'd kicked the tail of the town halfwit up Main.'

Burdin said nothing but even with the dim light

Ronan could see the wariness thicken in his beady, almost lashless eyes.

'That makes you a mighty miserable son of a bitch in my eyes, Burdin. Don't think I can take to you at all.'

On the last word, Matt Ronan slammed the side of his six-gun into Trace's flabby gut. The man gagged and his knees sagged as he grabbed at himself. Ronan whipped his Colt barrel across the man's bullet head, twice each way, and by the time Burdin's knees struck the ground and he started to stretch out, he was spitting bloody teeth. He didn't move as his face ploughed into the dirt.

Denby started to scramble to his feet and Ronan whirled, clubbed him across the back of the head, knocking him sprawling. Breathing hard, Denby twisted and began to crab away backwards, using hands and boots, backside dragging through the dirt.

'Hold it,' Ronan told him and when Denby didn't obey he put a bullet between the man's boots.

Denby yelled and stopped dead, whitefaced. 'N-now wait up! You just wait up! You dunno who you're messin' with here!'

'Sure I do. You're the belly-draggin' snake who crushed my hand with a rock.'

Denby's swallow was clearly audible. His mouth opened but no words came until he cleared his throat. 'W-what're you – gonna do?'

Ronan pursed his lips thoughtfully. 'By my calculations, I've got one bullet left in my Colt.'

'You – you kill me and Pa'll never give up till he runs you down! I mean it! He—'

The rest of Denby Cline's words were lost in the gunshot and the man's high-pitched scream as Ronan's last bullet smashed through his right hand.

His body convulsed and he snatched it against his chest, lying back, writhing and rolling about, groans and curses mingling with his sobs of pain. Denby cringed as Ronan holsterd his six-gun and stepped forward. He yanked the neckerchief from around Denby's neck and dropped it into his lap. The man, out of his head with pain, stared at it, and then the girl handed her rifle to Ronan, knelt and swiftly tied the cloth around the bleeding hand. Denby passed out with the pain as the cloth pressed firmly against shattered bones protruding through the bullet-torn flesh.

She looked at Ronan as she stood up, half smiling.

'I knew you good man.'

CHAPTER 9

DEADLY BONUS

Jesse Cline looked up irritably from his ledger as a sweating man stepped into his office at the wheel works after a peremptory knock.

'Goddammit, Herm, haven't I told you never to charge in here like a loco steer? And you know what happens to loco steers!'

Breathless, Herm, wide-eyed said, 'S-sorry, boss – b-but they just brought in Denby and Trace.'

Jesse felt a shift in his belly, a tightening of the muscles and the involuntary clenching of his hands. 'The hell d'you mean, "just brought 'em in"? What's wrong with 'em?'

He was already on his feet, moving fast towards the door, reading dire news in the face of the sweating clerk.

He pushed past the man and turned into the work-shop section, seeing men gathering in the big double doorway there. Two wagons were being worked on but the men had put down their tools and joined others at the door, bunching around some horses. His son and foreman were being helped down and he blanched when he saw Denby's hand with the crudely-applied blood-soaked bandages. Trace Burdin seemed stunned, standing there with his big arms dangling at his sides, a slight glaze in his eyes, smashed lips, battered face.

'What the hell. . . ?'

They sat Denby down on an upturned nail keg and Trace was led a few feet away and seated on a wagon shaft, shoulders slumped. Jesse frowned at the ramrod but turned to Denby, grey-faced, who was rocking gently holding his right arm across his chest.

'I asked what the hell happened?' Jesse roared.

Denby flinched. 'Trace an' me, we had a few drinks in town last night, figured we'd shoot up the breed's cabin on the way home,' Denby said in a low voice, words interspersed with grunts and moans. 'Goddamn bitch shot my hoss from under me, put Trace afoot, too. Ronan, Ronan put a bullet through my gunhand, busted it up all to hell an' gone. Look, Pa—'

He started to unravel the bandage and Jesse snapped: 'Leave it be, you fool! It's bleedin' bad. What's wrong with Trace? He still drunk?'

'Ronan gun-whipped him somethin' awful, Pa. Thought his skull was cracked. Aw, Jesus, Pa, I – I've never had such pain!'

'Mebbe you can compare it with Ronan.

Goddammit, I told you *I'd* decide when to shoot up the cabin! I wanted 'em to settle in, feel all nice an' comfy, then I aimed to hit 'em. Ah, get 'em across to Doc Swanston's and someone better get Jack Ifield, though I guess there won't be much he can do, with no witnesses from Delta to back your story.'

'We could get a few of the boys to say they was with Den, boss,' suggested one of the men.

'Could we? You'd find witnesses who saw them in town, drinking with Denby, I suppose, when everyone and his brother knows Delta C men aren't allowed off the ranch except Saturdays, and then on roster. Go get these two fixed up.'

'Aw, Pa, we just thought it'd help. . . .'

'You didn't think, that's always been your trouble, Denby. Go on. See what Swanston has to say.'

Doc Swanston didn't have much to say even as he worked on the wreckage of Denby's hand. He had given the man a high dose of laudanum and, combined with the remnants of the whiskey he had consumed the night before, Denby Cline was away with the fairies, muttering, half-smiling, *yelling* in wild pain.

'What's the verdict, Doc?' growled Jesse who had reluctantly left his office to come see for himself what damage Ronan had done.

'Not *quite* as bad as what Denby did to Matt Ronan's hand with a rock, but the outlook of a return to normal use of his right hand is no better than Ronan's.'

'Damn you, Doc! You just sayin' that because you're on Ronan's side?'

'I'm on the side of Medicine, Jesse, with a capital "M". The bullet has smashed the small bones and literally ripped out nerves. No one on this earth that I know of can replace them.'

Jesses scowled. 'What about Trace?'

'Burdin? Well, I'm afraid I must be most unprofessional and say that someone should have gunwhipped him long ago. The man's a sadist and has gotten away with his misdeeds for too long without any kind of retribution.'

'What're you sayin'? That's he's gonna die? He's gonna be lame-brained? What?'

'Unfortunately, he will recover. It may take a little time but he will probably be meaner and more short-tempered than ever.'

Jesse Cline grunted. 'Well, forget Trace. You do what you have to, but *after* you do all you can for Denby.'

'All I can do for Denby is clean the wound, bandage the hand and put it in a plaster cast, just as I was restricted to those same things with Matt Ronan.' Swanston allowed himself a faint, crooked smile. 'There is a certain poetic justice involved here, I believe.'

'What you better *believe*, Doc, is that if you don't do your absolute best for my son, you'll be out of business – permanent.'

'Thank you, Jesse, that is about what I expected you to say. Now you can go, and take your friends with you. I'll keep Trace and Denby here for a spell, in the infirmary. You'll get my bill in due course.'

Cline leaned forward, thrust his reddened face close to the startled medic's. 'You said that wrong, Doc. Not "Trace and Denby"; it's *"Denby and Trace"*, and you keep it that way!'

Doc felt sweat break out on his brow and in his armpits as the big man stormed out, followed by his crew.

With a sigh, he turned towards the moaning Denby.

Jack Ifield looked uncomfortable as he stared across his desk at the near-apoplectic Jesse Cline.

'Well, Jesse, it's gonna be hard to prove anythin'. I mean, in the dark, no one there but Denby, Trace, Ronan, and the 'breed woman . . .' he spread his hands and shrugged. 'No witnesses, see? Ronan and the squaw tell their story, Den and Trace, theirs, and there's no one to back either pair.'

'Christ almighty! What the hell're you pullin'? You know Ronan put a bullet through Denby's hand! You know who to believe, dammit!'

'Well, I believe Trace and Den – I reckon they're tellin' the truth – but, hell, Ronan and the squaw had every right to defend themselves.'

Jesse sneered. 'You yellow-gutted snake! After all the backing I've given you since I got you this job!'

'Well, Jesse, I don't reckon you can complain about the kinda backin' I gave *you* in all that time. Judas, I do whatever you tell me, well, most times, but this is one of them things that if Seamus O'Malley buys in – and he will, Doc Swanston'll see to that – O'Malley'll wipe the floor with it, rub our noses in the dirt. You know that, Jesse.'

Jesse's thick forefinger stabbed the air right under Ifield's nose so fast and close that the sheriff reared back and almost toppled out of his chair.

'*Right*!' Cline yelled. 'You better start lookin' for another job. Don't you worry about it not being election year; I can fix it so you lose this job before sundown if I work at it! You think about that!'

The words lashed Ifield like a whip but he made one more try. 'Jesse, if you don't control your men someone else'll get hurt – and they'll send a marshal down from Dodge.'

'You're right, Jack – about one thing. Someone else *will* get hurt. You're damn right about that.' Cline slammed out, looking as if he hoped to come across a raging grizzly just so he could take a poke at it.

Ifield sat there despondently: he knew Cline wasn't bluffing about taking his job from him. He turned towards his file cabinet, brushed aside a batch of folders and brought out a flat bottle of whiskey.

He needed a drink – a big one.

At the same time as Jack Ifield took his first swig from the flat bottle, Jesse Cline propped in the middle of Main Street as a man riding a dusty roan gelding and leading a laden packhorse, almost ran him down.

'Watch where the hell you're goin', damn you!'

The rider, who had been obviously dozing in the saddle, covered with almost as much trail dust as his mount, jerked awake and scrubbed a hand around his stubbled face.

'Well, pardon me all to hell, *amigo*, I guess I dozed off. Ah, it's Mr Cline, right?'

Jesse squinted against the bright sunlight. 'I know you?'

'We met briefly, some weeks back when you fixed my chuckwagon's front wheel. Skip Barlow.'

'Ah, yeah. Hardly recognized you through all that dirt. Get a good price for your herd in Dodge?'

'Top of the ladder, first herd in of the season.'

'Damn well pipped me at the post there,' Cline growled. 'My herd wasn't ready, isn't yet, owing to a few things I have no control over.'

'Wouldn't be a touch of tick fever, would it?'

Jesse grunted. 'You damn Texans are to blame for the spread of that! Aah, to hell with it. I'll have it beat in another few weeks. Market ought to hold up that long.' He stepped around the packhorse and continued on his way, striding long and heavy, a bad mood hunching his shoulders.

'Hey, Cline, which street I take to Doc Swanston's? I'm kinda tuckered and turned-around some. Been a long, long trail.'

Jesse pointed to Mulberry Street without looking or pausing, striding back towards his own building.

'Well, *muchas gracias*,' Barlow said sourly and nudged his horses towards the cross street just ahead, stifling a yawn.

*

Doc Swanston hardly recognized Skip Barlow when he arrived with all the dust and grit plastering him. The trail herder stood on the side porch and slapped himself down with his crumpled hat.

The doctor stepped out, waving a hand in front of his face, coughing. 'You might have left the trail outside . . . good Lord! Mr Barlow, isn't it?'

'Yeah, sorry, Doc, but I've had a long hard ride from Dodge. Had to take a few side trails and, well, there were a couple of hardcases after me that required some attention. Haven't had time to stop and get cleaned up.'

'We-ell, are you hurt? Wounded. . . ?'

'No, no – I'm OK. I managed to drive 'em off.' He seemed as if he would add something else but then changed his mind. 'I guess by now Matt Ronan's been discharged?'

'He has – not with a great deal of improvement, and yet at the same time I am amazed he has recovered as well as he has.'

Barlow seemed impatient, his eyes reddened from the trail and lack of sleep. 'You know where he is?' As Doc hesitated, he added, 'I've got his trail pay for him, and a bonus.'

'That's generous of you.'

Barlow grunted. 'Got a good price for my steers and upset Jessse Cline into the bargain. Where'll I find Matt?'

'I sent him up to some land I'm holding in trust.

It's out in the foothills but . . . there's been a little trouble.' He stood aside. 'Come inside, you might be interested in this.'

'Well, Doc, I'm in kind of a hurry to see Ronan.'

But Swanston was already moving down the passage and Barlow followed, dust falling from him in a small cloud as he clumped into the infirmary. He stopped as Swanston gestured to two occupied beds in a corner, peered more closely and recognized Denby Cline and Trace Burdin, whose head was swathed in bandages, his face war-painted with iodine over several cuts.

'I see by that sling and the plaster cast that somethin' bad's happened to Denby's hand . . . I'm glad to say. Would I be out of line to say that I'm hoping it's a payback for what Denby did to Ronan?'

Swanston smiled crookedly. 'That's not very charitable, but, yes. Denby was over-confident, thought Ronan would be an easy target. His mistake – Ronan put a bullet through the back of Denby's hand, made a terrible mess of it, almost as bad as that rock that crushed his own hand.'

Barlow smiled. 'Then he might be mighty pleased to get the bonus I've brought him.'

Swanston frowned. 'I'm not sure I understand.'

'You wouldn't, Doc. But if you'll tell me how to find Matt, I'll make a quick trip to the bath house then take it to him. I know damn well he'll be mighty happy to get it.'

'Well, I'm not so sure money means much to Matt.'

'It's not money, Doc – more like a life-saver.'

CHAPTER 10

FIVE OR SIX

Barlow heard the shooting as he entered the foothills according to Doc Swanston's directions.

'Leave the regular trail at a bend where there's a boulder up the slope that resembles a huge cow skull or, some say, a buffalo's head, though I can't see that myself. You'll need to take care going down a very steep slope, but it will bring you out to a flat area, and at the western end a rise begins. Skirt it and you'll see the cabin and lean-to through a screen of trees. A careful rider could make his way almost to the back door without being seen.'

Barlow had frowned slightly at that, looking more like his old self now he had bathed and bought fresh clothes. He rubbed a hand over his freshly shaved jowls. 'Why not ride in from the front. . . ?'

'You saw Denby and Trace Burdin; you probably don't know Jesse Cline very well, but he's not the sort who will sit twiddling his thumbs after something as drastic as that smashed-up hand of Denby's. He will want revenge, and as he nurses a hatred for Indians, of whatever gender or age. . . . Plus your little upset about the trail herd. . . .'

'I get it, Doc, thanks. I'll be on my way.'

'I almost wish I could come with you. I think I'd like to see Matt's reaction to your, er, bonus.'

And Swanston had been right, judging by the gunfire: Barlow would bet it was some of Jesse's hard-cases from Delta C rousting Ronan and the Indian girl.

So he decided to approach from the rear and, if necessary – and he rather hoped it *would* be necessary – buy into any fracas on behalf of the besieged pair.

His horse had benefited from the brief stopover in Skywater, too, having been curry-combed, fed some oats and even had a new soft blanket tucked under the trail-worn saddle. So the roan did not protest as Barlow urged it up the steep slope after the long slide down from the regular trail.

The shooting was sporadic and came from higher up the big slope, but that was all to the good, because the bulk of the main cabin would give him cover as he closed in.

Then suddenly there were wild yells and the whinnying of roughly-handled mounts, and an increase in gunfire. Barlow swore; he knew the sounds meant whoever was doing most of the shooting was now moving in on the cabin in a wild charge. Perhaps it might be a last raking volley before riding off, but more likely it was an attempt at gaining entry to the cabin, or throwing blazing torches on to the dry shingle roof.

He could smell pinewood smoke which is what made him think of this last, and then his spurs dug into the roan's flanks and it gave a startled whinny of protest. He hoped it wouldn't be heard by the raiders above – probably not, with all the racket they were making.

Stiffly, Barlow leaned back and yanked and tugged at a bedroll behind the cantle, flipping out the edge of a blanket covering one end. Straining a little, from his awkward angle, he groped for the object he was looking for.

He grinned tightly as he found it and let out a wild Apache war cry: 'And I don't care a pinch of possum poop whether you hear it or not! 'Cause in a minute, what you're gonna hear will put the fear of God into you!'

The well-muscled roan fairly flew up the slope and skidded slightly as it went round the north end of the cabin. . . .

There were six or seven raiders, storming down from the heights, most shooting wildly with rifles and six-guns, but two men carried blazing branches and it was obvious the men with guns were giving them covering fire while they rode in and tried to toss the torches on to the cabin roof.

Lily had been doing most of the shooting with the

rifle and had earlier brought down one raider's horse, then almost immediately shot him off the mount he'd swung aboard with the aid of its rider helping him up behind. That seemed to be the signal for the men to start their charge on the cabin and they were intent on making Ronan and the Indian girl keep their heads down as they swept in, peppering the already bullet-pocked walls.

'I'm low on ammo,' Ronan gritted even as the girl worked the Winchester's lever and also realized the magazine was empty. She answered but whatever she said was drowned in the sudden roar of a shotgun. Ronan jumped: the Delta C men hadn't used a shotgun before this!

The girl threw him a puzzled look, too, as the shotgun roared outside again, sounding closer. He crouched by the splintered window shutter, only three cartridges left in his pistol. His left hand was aching and his right was sore from banging it against things in his awkward hurry to shoot back at Jesse Cline's raiders.

'New man!'

He spun as the girl spoke the words, ducked a little lower to see through the splintered wood of the shutter and saw a man on a racing roan, its tail streaming, riding in from the north end of the cabin, *firing a shotgun from his shoulder.*

But this was no ordinary shotgun: it *looked* like the usual single- or double-barrelled Greener or whatever make it was, but the rider was doing something with his left hand, moving it swiftly under the barrel, back and forth, and an ejected shell case arced through the air, still smoking, as the gun thundered again. The hand blurred once more, a cartridge case flew up in front of the rider's face and yet another blast thundered immediately.

Two men were already reeling in the saddle and a third was fighting his mount that showed red streaks across its rump.

The other riders hauled rein, wheeled, as the shotgun roared yet again, and raced like the wind across the face of the slope. A full retreat.

'It's Barlow!' a puzzled Ronan said, standing now in the doorway as the raiders fled. He stepped outside and kicked a burning torch away from the cabin. The second torch was nowhere to be seen and he ran a little way up the slope so he could see the roof but there was no blazing branch on the shingles either. Maybe the rider who carried it had dropped it and it had extinguished itself. . . .

Then the raiders topped out over the crest and were gone. Barlow came riding back, the butt of his shotgun resting on his left thigh. He hauled rein and lifted his right hand to his hat brim.

'Howdy, ma'am. You, too, Matt. You're lookin' a lot more chipper than when I last saw you.'

'I'm damned glad to see you, no matter how you look.' Ronan pointed to the gun. 'What kinda hellish weapon is that you got there?'

Barlow swung down and grinned as he handed the gun to the curious Ronan.

'It's a Spencer-Bannerman slide-action shotgun,

one of only two in the Territory right now. Its twin is back in Dodge with the local law. I had a helluva time talking him round to selling me this one. It's such a good weapon, I even had three hard boys follow me outta town and try to take it off me.'

'They not so hard, I think,' said Lily flatly, pointing to the weapon. Barlow smiled thinly.

'Nope, not when I gave 'em a demonstration of what it can do. The first successful slide-action to go into production and hit the commercial market.'

Ronan was examining the gun now, the girl standing back but curious, too. 'I saw you fire four or five times.'

'It can shoot as many as six – magazine holds five shot shells, and you can put one in the breech too, after loading – up to you.'

Ronan indicated the wooden grip under the barrel, six or eight inches back from the muzzle. 'This the slide?'

'Yep. Work it and it feeds a shell into the breech, and keeps feedin' four or five more, and if you hold the trigger depressed while you're working the slide, it'll feed and fire till the magazine's empty: almost like a portable Gatling gun, if you're on the wrong end of it. But you'll figure it out and get used to it.'

Ronan snapped his head up. 'Me?'

'Yeah, a bonus for you. For helpin' stop that stampede back at Cripple Creek. I figured if Denby'd messed-up your gun hand, this might kind of compensate for it. Doc told me you might even be able to grip it with your right hand, and hold it steady enough for your left to work the slide. OK?'

Ronan glanced at the Indian girl who smiled faintly and he nodded, 'I reckon so! Yessir, Skip, I reckon it's a whole damn lot better'n just "OK"!'

Once they were certain the raiders had left and had taken their wounded with them, Lily made coffee and they sat at the deal table, now splintered at one end from a tumbling bullet. Barlow told them about his entrance to Dodge with the meathouse agent, and how they had arrived during the bank robbery.

'I rode in shootin' but the agent went the other way. I nailed one feller – turned out there was a reward for him and that's what I used to buy that shotgun. I'd just seen the marshal come a'hellin' outta his office, usin' his, and he blew every one of them robbers outta their saddles in about twenty seconds. Couldn't b'lieve my eyes.'

'Must've been somethin to see.'

'Yeah, it was. Anyway, afterwards I went to see him and he showed me the gun – first one in Dodge, and he had a second one coming. The makers wanted *him* to use 'em, knowin' his rep. for taming towns because it'd give them plenty of publicity and help boost their sales.'

'What made you buy one for me?'

'Knew the trouble Denby'd left you with and I've gotten to know you well enough workin' for me to figure that you'd have to square with Denby. Seems you've done that, but he's bound to come after you, so you'll need a weapon you can handle, fast and deadly – that slide-action's it, I reckon.'

Ronan had the shotgun in his lap and hefted it, working the slide smoothly. There were no shells in the magazine and he felt quite comfortable handling the gun, though he almost dropped it twice.

The gap between his thumb and first finger on his clawed hand fitted the gooseneck of the stock as if designed for it. He could work the slide back and forth like a steam-driven piston with his left hand.

'There's no exposed hammer to worry about cocking for each shot,' Barlow pointed out. 'There's a spring-loaded locking bar in the top of the breech that engages and disengages with the action of the slide. As long as you keep the trigger depressed, you can pump away and fire and eject. You'll get really fast with practice.'

With his left hand working the slide speedily, pushing a shell into the breech, the gun would fire. Working the slide again would eject the used shell while replacing it with a fresh one and fire again, and so on until the magazine was empty. Barlow smiled as he saw the look on Ronan's face.

'Lucky the little finger on my right hand is the only one with any flexibility. See? It can reach the trigger easy, no trouble to hold it back while I work the slide.'

'Just keep that trigger depressed and you can get off five or six shots in about the time it takes to say your own name. Sam Colt's experimenting with a slide-action rifle called the Lightning that does the same thing, but it'll shoot even faster, the ammunition being smaller and quicker to load.'

'Skip, it's the answer to one mighty big problem for me. I dunno how the recoil will affect my bad hand but I'll have lots of practice until I get it right – and when I do—'

'You kill Denby – Jesse, too.'

Both men looked at Lily as she spoke: her face was set, her eyes hard, and Ronan knew she was remembering the bad time Cline and his men had given her previously, even when Marks was alive.

Ronan nodded. 'Yeah, don't reckon Jesse's gonna be content to let me keep walking around.'

Lily reached out and patted the blued barrel of the shotgun. 'Keep new friend with you.'

'That's good advice, Matt. The barrel's about thirty inches long, you can cut maybe six inches off that, but no more.' As Ronan arched his eyebrows, quizzically, Skip said, stifling a yawn, 'You have to load from the front, under the barrel. Cut too much off and you'll hack into the feeder tube. Best have a gunsmith do it.'

Ronan nodded, knowing he had a lot to learn about this strange, deadly weapon before he could use it effectively in any gunfight. Then a strange thing happened: one of his clawed fingers began to itch. It was the first time he had felt any other sensation in it except pain since Denby had crushed his hand.

In a normal hand, it would have been called his trigger finger.

Every time Jesse Cline saw Counsellor Seamus

O'Malley he could not prevent the surge of wonder at the man's appearance. He was possibly the most powerful man in the state of Kansas, held big-time ranchers and businessmen, even the occasional senator, in awe of his knowledge and application of the law of the land. He had ruined several men who figured they could oppose him, find loopholes to circumvent the letter of the law. He had hired and fired sheriffs and marshals in Dodge City as well as in Skywater. And when he pursed those wet, blubbery lips and pointed to the door, or to the end of Main Street where it spilled over at the edge of town into open trail, men hung their heads, smothered any curses they may have been harbouring, and went on their way.

O'Malley had 'authority' and had, in fact, very recently been appointed circuit judge for Southern Kansas.

He had never been known to wear a gun, although he carried an ivory-handled and silver-tipped ebony cane everywhere: more for show than practical use. Some folk maintained it was really a disguised firearm, but no one had seen him use it as such. His personality seemed powerful enough to make men obey, despite his small stature.

And that was what Jesse couldn't savvy: O'Malley was barely five feet four inches tall (if tall was the right word!) in his shoes, had a fifty-inch waist, a squeaky voice and the only hair on his head grew in tufts above his ears: a true comic figure. Jesse decided that it was the eyes that did it, made men obey without argument, for those orbs could have doubled for the muzzles of a twin-barrelled shotgun . . . or, when narrowed, the business ends of a pair of six-guns.

Like now: even Jesse felt the involuntary knotting of his stomach muscles as O'Malley glared at him across his desk, waving several pages in one of his pudgy, child-like hands.

'This, Mr Jesse Cline, is what is known as an injunction – taken out against you by the good Doctor Swanston sitting here at my right hand. It's for an unwarranted and patently dangerous attack on land held in trust by Doc Swanston and known as 'Marks' Domain' in the foothills of the Sunridge Range – as I believe you well know.'

'I never made any damn attack, warranted, unwarranted or otherwise! And that old sawbones knows it!' It was Jesse's turn to glare and he bored a bleak gaze towards Swanston's bland, composed face.

'Not you personally, Jesse,' Doc told him equably. 'Your men.'

'My men! Judas Priest, you think I can watch my men every blasted minute? I've got two businesses to run. If my crew go to town and get a few drinks under their belts, then, on the way home decide to kick over the traces a little, just for the hell of it, lettin' off a little steam—' He paused, shook his head vigorously. 'No, sir! You can't hold me responsible for that.'

'Can – will – and do,' snapped O'Malley with massive confidence, seeing Jesse's jaw drop. 'You are ultimately responsible for your crew's actions, Jesse, and don't pretend you're not aware of that. If you so wish, I can easily find it in print in one of my reference books.'

O'Malley gestured to the shelves lining the office walls, crammed with leather-bound books in various colours, all thick as a man's hand-span, they seemed almost threatening just by being there.

'Don't bother. But I wasn't even in the county when this alleged attack took place – and I can prove it.'

'Alleged?' snapped the usually calm medico. 'The cabin is like a sieve there are so many bullet holes: a miracle Lily wasn't injured. And the lean-to! Well, it wasn't much to begin with, but now it's virtually uninhabitable.'

Jesse smiled slyly. 'Then Ronan has a perfect excuse for moving in openly with that damn squaw! So what's he bitchin' about?'

O'Malley shook his head. He sighed. 'That's about the level of your intelligence, Jesse. Doc is describing the damage your men have caused.' He picked up another, smaller paper from his desk. 'Here is an estimate of the cost to repair the buildings and—'

'You're crazy!' Cline yelled, studying the figures. 'This is plumb ridiculous! Goddamn outrageous!'

'Those estimates were made by Linus Spalding himself and you know his reputation for honesty and accuracy, and as top man in building construction in three states – his home territory, of course, being this one.'

Jesse glared. 'You'll have to take me to court!'

'Yes,' Doc agreed easily. 'We're prepared for that.'

O'Malley smiled faintly. 'And you can add substantial court costs to those estimates, Jesse. You will lose, I assure you. And now, as I am officially circuit judge for this area, I can set this hearing up promptly or delay it until such time as it suits.' The smile broadened. 'Suits me, that is.'

Cline knew when he was beaten but it sure did not sit sweetly with him. He was pale and shaking with barely controlled rage. 'I can't come up with money like this! My credit's stretched with a new herd I'm buying and outfitting for a trail drive.'

'And I believe you have a mortgage on your wheelwright's business,' O'Malley said with a thin smile as Jesse gave him a startled look. 'Michael Allen, the banker, is my wife's cousin, if that's of any interest to you, Jesse.'

Cline crumpled the paper in his fist and flung it on the desk. 'The hell with both of you! I can't afford to pay this, and that's all there is to it!' He glared challengingly.

Unperturbed O'Malley said evenly, 'Then it's court, or . . .' O'Malley paused for effect, 'Perhaps if you gave your solemn word that there will be no more such attacks on the doctor's property, he might be content for you to lend him some of your men to help repair the damage they've done. . . ? Strictly speaking it is Water-Lily's property, or soon will be, and it could be good for your image, Jesse, if you were seen to be helping a disadvantaged person.'

'You mean use my men to rebuild that bitch's. . . !' Cline choked on the words.

'Much, much cheaper than going to court, Jesse,' O'Malley pointed out with his damnable smugness, knowing he held the high cards in his hand. 'And, Doc, of course, would expect you to take better control of your men and ensure that nothing of the sort ever happens again. If it does, someone could be badly hurt, and I'm not just talking about legal actions.'

Seething, Cline bored his red-eyed glare into the maddeningly calm face of the little man. 'You could damn well bet on that! But, all right, where are the papers? I know damn well you'll have 'em all ready.'

'Correct, Jesse.' O'Malley took several sheets of paper from his top desk drawer. He thrust them towards the trembling rancher.

Jesse broke two pen nibs before he produced an acceptable signature, glared wordlessly, then turned and stormed out.

'You're a marvel, Seamus,' Doc Swanston said, studying the signed copy O'Malley handed him. 'I didn't really think it would work.'

'With a man like Jesse Cline, you hit him in his hip pocket and he's putty in your hands.'

'In your hands, you mean, Seamus.'

O'Malley acknowledged this with a modest inclination of his cherub head.

CHAPTER 11

THUNDER IN
THE HILLS

Barlow stayed at the cabin with Lily while Ronan took the shotgun into town. He went to the only gunsmith Skywater boasted, a man named Sid Charlton. He was an Englishman, son of a famous gunsmith in a place called Sheffield, well-known for its knives and, apparently the high quality of its steel in general.

Ronan knew nothing about England and had a little trouble understanding Charlton's accent at first but he was impressed with the man's work and his immediate interest in the Spencer-Bannerman shotgun.

'I've read about this,' he said fondling the weapon. He was a big man with thick forearms like a blacksmith but his hands seemed gentle, as they moved over the shotgun, almost caressing the weapon. 'One

of the first truly successful slide-action shotguns. Fine
work – don't like interfering with it.'

Ronan held up his clawed hand. 'I'm stuck with
this, mister, and somehow I've got more enemies
than I need. I'd be obliged if you'd shorten the
barrel, but if it's not to your liking, I'll do it myself.'

Charlton looked horrified. 'No, no, no, no, no!'
he said emphatically. 'I think not. I will do it, and if I
may also suggest,' he paused and seemed reluctant to
go on, but added, 'you will find it somewhat out of
balance and maybe difficult to carry, if not to shoot
accurately. You see the natural grain in the wood at
the gooseneck? See how it sweeps in a curve, sug-
gesting a pistol grip? That is, if one were to continue
that curve right through to the underside of the
stock, removing most of the actual butt.'

Ronan looked at him sharply. 'I figured to use the
butt to brace against my hip to help steady it down.'

'Yes, acceptable. But it is *bulk* I was thinking about
and a tendency to kick in recoil once the fore-part of
the barrel is removed. However, the new grip will fit
the, er, shape your hand has acquired since your
injury. I believe it will afford you as firm a hold as possible, help keep your buckshot in a tight, lethal
pattern.'

Ronan smiled. 'You are mighty polite, Mr
Charlton, and you have persuaded me. You go ahead
and shape it as you think fit. Think you could have it
ready for me by mid-afternoon?'

Charlton tended to rear back at the suggestion
that he hurry his work but he had heard about the

trouble Ronan was having and slowly nodded. 'Your time limit is acceptable.'

While he was waiting, Ronan visited Doc Swanston and his wife, surprised to find both Trace Burdin and Denby Cline gone from the infirmary.

'Trace has a hard head and recovered quickly,' Doc told him. 'Denby tends to moan and groan a lot more than necessary but Jesse himself came in and demanded his discharge. I had the impression that he wants Denby back at Delta for some urgent reason.'

'You hinting that reason might be the Marks' land, Doc?'

'I have nothing solid to support my premonition, but yes. I think you should stay very much alert, Matt.'

'I thought O'Malley had Jesse nailed now with that injunction you took out?'

Doc frowned, looking uncomfortable. 'O'Malley can be relentless at times, get carried away with his own importance. *I* have the feeling that perhaps he went a shade too far, pushed Jesse to the edge. The man is so stretched financially right now that he can't afford any other worries to distract him. He may well run wild.'

'You sayin' he might make an all-out raid on Lily's place?'

Doc sighed. 'I said I had nothing tangible to go on. It sounds as if it would be a stupid move on Jesse's part but I believe he's past thinking rationally. He was a frightening figure the way he bullied Denby into agreeing to leave this place. I didn't get a chance to argue. Well, I may be too pessimistic, Matt, but, please take care, man.'

Ronan had decided he would heed the doctor's warning. The medic knew Jesse Cline and his moods and the way he might react, and Doc was no scare-monger.

He picked up the shotgun at the gunsmith's and was elated when he found the curve of the pistol grip the man had shaped for him: Charlton had filed a groove to take the notch between thumb and fore-finger so that his partly-working little finger could reach the trigger more easily and hold it depressed without difficulty. He had even added some checker-ing to give his hand a better grip, and Ronan knew he now had a weapon that would make it mighty hard for Jesse Cline and his crew to just walk in and take over Marks' Domain. There would be quite a few dead if they tried. . . .

Charlton had also 'taken the liberty' as he put it, and made a carry sling for the weapon: a simple arrangement of straps, rivetted, slung across his chest, a loop to hold the gun down at his left side with a swivel for fast shooting.

It was growing late but Ronan stopped at the diner to buy a slice of beefsteak pie and cake with dried fruit in it, then quit town, munching, heading for Lily's. fast.

He was perturbed to see how quickly the sun was being swallowed by a fiery sky. In the foothills it became dark as the shadows stretched along the trail and the prairie behind him.

Damn! He should have skipped that pie. He had meant to be back before dark. . . .

He urged his mount on and before the afterglow faded he was climbing fast towards Lily's cabin just over the next ridge. The outline of the big mountain behind her land looked solid against the glow of the rising moon.

Ronan hauled rein involuntarily, bringing a grunt of surprise and mild displeasure from the horse.

'Hell! That ain't moonrise, not in that direction! Looks more like a – a fire!'

You could blame Jack Ifield in a way. Or you could mark it up against Seamus O'Malley. Riding high on his new appointment as circuit judge, throwing his considerable weight around – as witness the way he had sent Jesse Cline into a tailspin – he sent a curt message to Sheriff Jack Ifield that he wanted to see him – at once.

Upon the lawman's arrival, without preamble, O'Malley held up a sealed envelope almost tiredly, as if it weighed a few pounds instead of ounces. 'Deliver this into Jesse Cline's hands only, and do it today. Not tomorrow or any other time – today. You understand, Jack?'

The small eyes lifted to the startled sheriff's face as the lawman automatically took the long, legal envelope with O'Malley's personal seal on the flap, a folded paper held in place on the outside with a

114

rubber band. 'Er, what is it, Counsellor?'

' "Judge" if you will from now on, Jack. It's Jesse's properly notarized and recorded copy of Doc Swanston's injunction taken out against him. As I said, I want it in Jesse's hands tonight, and I want you to bring me the receipt. Jesse is out at the ranch so you'll have to hurry.'

Jack was sweating and yet his mouth was dry as dust. He shuffled his feet. 'Hell, Coun— Judge, Jesse'll likely kick me down the stairs! He's mightily pissed off over this injunction deal and if I'm the one to give it to him—'

'It's part of your sworn duty as a representative of the law, Jack,' O'Malley snapped. 'Now get it done.'

'Listen, Judge! I mean it, Jesse'll likely take out his temper on me and—'

'As I said, it's part of your sworn duty as sheriff, Jack,' O'Malley cut in acidly. 'Jesse Cline may be able to put you out of a job but, if you don't follow my instructions, *I* will not only put you *out* of a job, I will put you *in* prison for a considerable time, six months minimum, if memory serves me correctly: refusal to carry out a judicial order being equivalent to *contempt of court*, you see? Now, show some good sense and deliver that injunction to Jesse and bring me the signed receipt – that's it attached to the envelope with a rubber band. On your way.'

O'Malley dismissed the unhappy sheriff with a wave of a pudgy hand towards the door and returned to the small pile of legal-looking documents in front of him on his ornate desk.

Chin down on his chest, Jack Ifield shuffled out, putting the injunction in a pocket of his vest, his stomach churning.

He was right: Jesse Cline blew up when Jack sat his lathered horse at the foot of Delta C's porch steps and waved the legal envelope.

'You only gotta sign the receipt and give it to me, Jesse.'

'You think so?' roared Cline, Denby and Trace Burdin now appearing behind him, the latter holding a shotgun. 'That goddamn doctor's got a surprise comin' and so has that squirt of a counsellor.'

'He's a circuit judge now, Jesse, and he can put you in jail if you don't stay clear of Ronan and that squaw.'

Jesse shook his head savagely, momentarily lost for words. 'I don't care if he's Jesus H. Christ! I've had a bellyful!' He rounded on Denby making the man jump and grab at his plastered and bandaged hand quickly. 'You started this! Couldn't be satisfied you'd beat Ronan unconscious, you had to smash up his gunhand with a rock!'

'Well, hell, Pa, he'd killed Farley!'

'Hell is what Ronan brought to this range thanks to you, and now he's got back-up with this trail driver and—'

'Jesse!' broke in Jack Ifield. 'You gonna sign? I gotta get back to O'Malley before dark and—'

'Goddammit! Will you shut up, or get the hell outta here! You're no damn good to me. I put you in

116

the sheriff's job and now you let someone like that pipsqueak O'Malley buffalo you and—'

'He can throw us all in jail, goddammit!' Jack broke in frantically. 'You've already signed the paper – he just wants a receipt to say that you've got it. Can't you show some sense and get the damn thing done so I can—'

'Who the hell you think you're talkin' to!'

Jesse's face was dark with surging blood and he snatched the shotgun from the startled Burdin and swung it towards Ifield who pulled the reins in tight against his body as he started to turn his mount away.

It could have been mistaken for a move towards his six-gun. . . .

The shotgun roared, both barrels, and Jack Ifield's body was hurled out of the saddle, the horse whinnied and shied and ran off. Denby and Burdin stared, not at the broken body of the sheriff, but at Jesse and the smoking gun.

'We're in a helluva lot of trouble now, boss,' Trace murmured, rearing back as Jesse rounded on him.

'Who says we are?'

'Well, you just killed a *sheriff*, Pa! A lawman, even if he wasn't much damn use, but still a lawman! O'Malley'll have a federal marshal down here in nothin' flat!'

Jesse frowned and the others saw the worry replace the hot-blooded anger on his sweating face. He stared, lips slightly parted, slowly shifted his gaze towards Ifield.

'We can't have him found here,' he said very

117

quietly, and looked down at the shotgun he still held. He thrust it back at Burdin who stepped away, shaking his head.

'I don't want it, boss!'

'You'll take it if I say so!'

'No.'

As Jesse raised the gun, with the obvious intention of using it to hit his ramrod, Denby suddenly spoke up.

'Pa, Ronan uses a shotgun now. If Jack was found on the squaw's land. . . .'

It took Jesse a moment or two to see the possibilities and then he grinned tightly. 'Hell, I raised me a son with a brain after all! *Yeah*! Perfect. In fact what could be more perfect?'

'Well,' said Denby slowly, feeling a rising excitement now. 'I – I can tell you, Pa, I been thinkin' about that land a lot, lyin' there in that damn infirmary. If you're willin' to take a chance, we can get that damn squaw – and Ronan – off that land for keeps.'

Jesse snapped his head up, frowning. 'What're you sayin', boy?'

'I already said it, Pa. You – you seem on the edge of tellin' O'Malley to go to hell, well I got a way of doin' it that'll get you off the hook and we'll come out smellin' like roses.' He suddenly wet a forefinger with his tongue and held it up, twisting it this way and that, smiling when he had it to his liking. 'Even the wind's blowin' in the right direction.'

Jesse frowned. 'For what?'

Denby smiled. 'To blow the smoke from our brandin' fire, which we'll set up just inside our line at that narrow-neck where you can step clear across Heartbreak Creek on to Lily's land, right down the slope from that cabin.'

'Christ! You can't think you'll smoke 'em out with a fire only big enough to heat a branding iron!'

'No, but if it kinda got outta control and set the brush alight, it'd jump the creek at that point, about where the grass is thick and lush because Lily don't run but a handful of cows. There'd be lots of smoke then.'

'Uh-huh. And when we did our duty and tried to stop the fire spreadin', wouldn't surprise me none if the squaw and her men opened fire on us, thinkin' we was attacking.'

'And we'd naturally have to defend ourselves!'

Denby's smiled widened, eyes opening innocently. 'Why of course, Pa. We couldn't just stand still and be shot at, could we?'

'Den, I was gonna write you outta my will. Now you can look forward to one day ownin' all of Delta C.'

'*And* the wheel repair business, Pa, OK?'

Jesse's smile tightened but he nodded. 'OK!'

'We better wrap Jack in a tarp or somethin',' Trace Burdin said. 'He's bleedin' somethin' awful on our ground.'

'Right!' snapped Jesse. 'Let's get started. Den, you go fetch Curly and Buzz and bring half a dozen mavericks. Trace and me'll set up the brandin' fire. Now move! I want this over before dark!'

119

*

And by the time darkness fell on that side of the mountain, there was a massive wall of fire sweeping up towards Lily's cabin, driven not only by the evening wind, but by the hot-air currents of its own making.

The smoke made an effective screen for the Delta C riders to close in with guns blazing.

CHAPTER 12

GONE

They didn't know that Ronan wasn't in the cabin.

But the rifle fire soon had them wondering why there were no shotgun blasts; they expected Matt Ronan would be using his new weapon.

The attackers – there were six of them – wore bandannas across their faces, not to disguise their identities so much as to save breathing in the thick roiling clouds of smoke from the fire that was now devouring the mountain.

Horses in the corrals were screaming and pawing at the rails, terrified, even though the flames were still yards away. The heat came in a blasting wall that seemed almost solid; sparks and burning twigs fell like rain.

Crouched by a window, Barlow looked sharply at Lily. 'I'll have to turn the broncs loose! That damn fire could well reach here with the wind behind it!'

The wind flattened the grass on the slope, shook the branches in the young trees even as they burned.

Lily, face flushed, thumbing cartridges into her rifle, nodded, didn't take her gaze off the slope she could barely see through the smoke beyond the window. There were no clear target; just shapeless shadows flitting here and there, some mounted, some afoot . . . *all* with blazing auns. But already two had been wounded for certain – hopefully more.

She glanced at Barlow then as he unlatched the back door and prepared to make the short run to the corral to throw down the gate bar. 'Go fast, Bar-low!'

Then her rifle was blazing in a rapid volley that scattered the ghostly shapes in the smoke. When the magazine was empty, a return volley had her ducking low while she fumbled new cartridges into her rifle. Splinters flew and rained down on her dark hair and shoulders. She willed her slim hands to stop shaking so much, but her heart was pounding against her ribs so that it sounded like a drumbeat in her head.

While the raiders kept shooting at Lily's window, Barlow went through the door in a headlong dive, shoulder-rolling to one side, keeping a corner of the bullet-riddled cabin between him and the attackers. He leapt up, fell into a crouch almost at once, lunged for the gate bar.

Something slammed into his body like a runaway steer and hurled him on to his side in the dust. The world exploded in crimson and gold, with a swiftly falling black curtain. But he reached up and knocked the gate bar's locking wedge free. Gasping, straining, he fell forward, using his weight to thrust open the gate.

The horses, shrilling, manes and tails streaming, rushed out. He grunted involuntarily as he was sent spinning, panic-driven hoofs pounding his body into the ground.

Matt Ronan rode into what looked like a battlefield – thick smoke, thundering flames ten feet high. He had the slide-action shotgun ready, still clipped to the unfamiliar sling swivel, holding it awkwardly in his clawed hand on his thigh, using his good hand to work the reins.

A rider came charging out of the smoke, saw him and wheeled, throwing down with his smoking six-gun. Ronan didn't recognize him – it was Buzz, from Delta C – but the threat of the gun was enough. His knees gripped the racing horse and, a shell already in the breech, he hooked his finger around the trigger, depressed it and held it there even as the gun thundered, muzzle rearing with the recoil.

The upward swing of the barrel naturally angled the charge of buckshot and Buzz literally lost his head, his jerking body disappearing swiftly into the wall of smoke.

A bullet burned across Ronan's cheek and he reeled, felt himself go past the point of balance, and jerked his boots free of the stirrups as the horse leaned over in a wild turn. He kicked away from the lunging animal, hit hard on the slope but luckily landed on his left shoulder. It hurt as he rolled and skidded, twisting wrenchingly on to his stomach. The slope dropped steeply here and with little effort he reared up to his knees. The gun was at his side, still on its swivel, and he gripped it in an instant.

A rider was thundering in, ready to finish him off. Ronan held the trigger depressed, worked the slide twice. The blasts shook him and he had to put down his left hand to keep from falling. Through the smoke he saw the would-be killer – the Delta C hand named Curly – blown out of the saddle. The racing horse flew by and almost collided with him.

He was sliding downslope now. There was a man below – he was sure it was Jesse Cline. He fumbled the shotgun across his chest, moving his crippled hand with difficulty, shoulder hurting with the awkwardness of the effort. Jesse, wide-eyed, crouched over his horse's neck, flung his arm outwards and back, triggering two fast, wild shots from the six-gun he held. Matt's gun bellowed its thunder; a spray of buckshot just caught Cline's upper arm, twisting his big body, but doing little more than sting, and draw a dozen or so beads of blood. Another Delta rider broke from the brush, one arm dangling, intent only on saving his own hide.

Ronan brought up with a jerk as he crashed into a bush that was almost burned away by now. It snapped under his weight and he fell on to his belly. Spitting dirt, he thrust up with a gritted roar of pain, sat back and worked the shotgun's slide again. It thundered and he rocked in his precarious position. The charge of buckshot whistled away into the dispersing smoke.

Now the fire was dying and had destroyed most of the brush. The cabin up-slope was burning at one end of the roof; the fire seemed to have a good hold.

Gasping, he staggered to his feet, whistling his mount to him as he saw Jesse disappearing around a knoll, running his horse hard. Matt grabbed a stirrup as his mount came to him. It half-dragged him up-slope, body wrenching painfully. The smoke had cleared a lot and he saw a body lying just outside the swinging gate of the small corral.

It was Barlow, bleeding badly from a bullet wound, but mostly from a bloody gouge that exposed a couple of his ribs under mangled flesh, no doubt caused by the hoof of one of the fleeing mounts.

Ronan snapped his head towards the cabin, called hoarsely, throat burning from the smoke, '*Lily! Lily!*'

He jumped when Barlow said in a strangled voice, just below where he stood. 'She's gone. They . . . took her. . . .'

Ronan felt his skin prickle with cold shock. 'Who?'

'D-Denby and . . . Trace. Dunno what happened to Jesse.'

'He's hightailing it back to Delta, I reckon. Never mind him! Where'd those sonuvers take Lily?'

Barlow, wincing as Ronan tried to staunch the blood with Barlow's wadded kerchief and his own, shook his head. 'D-dunno, but one of 'em called to the other, somethin' about a place called Redmount.'

'Seems funny they'd mention it. Almost like they wanted someone to know it could be where they're taking her.'

Barlow was drifting in and out of consciousness with the pain and now he looked straight up into Ronan's dirt-smeared face, eyes straining.

'You! It's a trap! For you! Follow, an' one of 'em'll be waitin' . . . to nail you!'

'Could be. You better lay quiet. I'll have to get you back to Doc Swanston.'

'No, get after Lily. That Burdin, he's an animal.'

'And you're dead if you don't get some proper medical help. So shut up and quit playin' hero. You're goin' to Doc Swanston. Nothin' we can do to save the cabin.'

Ronan stood shakily and looked around through the smoke, eyes streaming, but finding clear spaces now where he could see reasonably well.

'Lucky you freed the horses. Fire'll burn itself out; once past the cabin there's not much vegetation.'

'Dammit! Helluva deal for Lily, eh? Just gotta stand by an' lose it all!'

'Mebbe the wind'll drop. After I get you to the doc's I'll go after the others.' He paused, knelt again to tighten the crude bandage torn from Barlow's shirt, leaving the Texan in his blood-stained under-shirt.

'Jack Ifield's body's down the slope – been almost cut in two by a shotgun. Way he's lying, it's almost like someone stretched him out just clear of the fire.'

'Like, like they wanted him . . . noticed?'

'Could be. Pretty damn queer. Anyway, it's a long ride to the doc's: I'll have to rope you into the saddle,

Skip. Better practice gritting your teeth, pardner.'

There was no answer. Barlow had passed out.

Seamus O'Malley opened his front door, face tight with displeasure at being interrupted at his supper. He glared at the dishevelled Jesse Cline, holding a bloody left upper arm as he stood in the wedge of lamplight.

'What in the devil's happened to you?'

Cline gulped, gasping, making his chest heave more than it needed to, putting on the best act he could for O'Malley. He tried to sound genuinely distressed.

'Counsellor, there's—'

'*Judge!*' O'Malley corrected him curtly.

'Yeah, OK. All hell's busted loose out on the range.' Jesse waited but there was no reply, no hint of sympathy. O'Malley's cherubic face showed little interest. 'We were brandin' mavericks by Heartbreak Creek; one kicked up hell and scattered the fire. Grass caught and the wind took it across the creek on to that squaw's place.'

At last O'Malley's gaze sharpened. 'The Marks land?'

Jesse nodded. 'Wasn't our fault. We tried to put it out but they started shootin' at us. Musta thought we lit it on purpose.'

'Now, I wonder whatever would give them that idea?'

Jesse ignored the sarcasm. 'That squaw and Ronan and the goddamn Texan, all of 'em shootin' at us!

Ronan almost cut Jack Ifield in two with that damn shotgun of his. It was cold-blooded murder.' He lifted one side of his hand on his upper arm, showing the small amount of blood. 'Winged me, too, and I had to make a run for it.'

Still no sympathy from O'Malley. 'What was Jack Ifield doing at a maverick branding?'

'Lookin' for me. He'd missed me at the house. Said he had some paper you wanted me to sign. He just arrived as the fire got outta hand.' He shrugged. 'Wrong place, wrong time, I guess.'

'For somebody!' O'Malley snapped.

'Well, I just wanted to get it straight with you – Judge.' Jesse looked over his shoulder. 'That damn Ronan! Chased me off with his shotgun. Dunno where he is now. I better get Doc to look at this arm, then get back and see who else the sonuver's killed.'

'How long since all of this started?'

'Aw, hell, I dunno. Couple, three hours. Before full sundown.'

'Mmmm, I saw Matt Ronan leaving the gunsmith's earlier. I doubt he'd have been at Lily Marks' place by the time you say the shooting started.'

Jesse stiffened. 'I ain't lyin', Judge! He was there! Blazin' away with that damn sawed-off shotgun or whatever he uses. He could've killed us all like he nailed Jack Ifield.'

O'Malley started to speak: 'I suppose I'd better arrange for Jack's body to be brought in.'

But Jesse had turned away quickly and mounted, riding off without further word or delay.

He had got his story across where it counted, anyway. He'd stick to it, too, hell or high water! Who cared if Ronan was seen here? A man could make it out there in the time he claimed. Ah! Let the damn squaw try to explain it!

Jack Ifield was dead and that was what would count in the end . . . that, and who killed him.

'Only the bitch won't be around to say "yea" or "nay",' he told himself with a tight grin as he turned the weary horse towards Doc Swanston's. 'An', with luck, nor will Ronan! No witnesses, so they'll just have to take my word!'

CHAPTER 13

NO CHOICE

It took Ronan a lot longer to get Barlow into Skywater than he had reckoned on. Clouds slid across the waning moon, changing the light constantly.

Barlow was roped in the saddle, murmuring unintelligibly, upper body swaying: Matt hadn't been able to anchor him as well as he would have liked, handicapped as he was with his crippled arm.

The horses loping along side by side, he glimpsed wetness showing on the moaning Texan's bandaged side and knew the wound was still bleeding. He had no choice but to stop and tend to it.

He cut up his blanket and made a thick pad to cover the wound – the bullet hole was lost somewhere amongst that hoof-torn flesh – and wrapped the strips of blanket around as tightly as possible, giving Barlow's ribs better support. He had to use his teeth to tie the knots but they held better this time. He spat away the lousy taste, scrubbing his lips.

The trail driver still swayed about but at least his bandages were now firm and contained the bleeding better.

Just the same, Ronan was glad to see the scattered lights of Skywater and made his way to the doctor's house through side streets once he was in the town proper.

Swanston helped him get Barlow inside and unwrapped the bandages. They were sodden and the Texan looked grey, his rugged face drawn. Swanston leaned down to examine the wound better, his wife gently pushing Ronan aside so as to hold the lamp closer for illumination.

'Reckon he'll make it, Doc?'

'He's *an hombre muy duro*, as they say where he comes from – Tough, with a capital "T". I reckon he'll pull through; I'll know better once I see how deep the bullet's penetrated.' He prepared his instruments and Mrs Swanston bustled about with hot water and antiseptics.

'They've got Lily, Doc.' Both Swanstons froze briefly and Matt went on to explain succinctly what he knew of the little slice of hell that had happened at Marks' Domain. 'Jesse set it up OK but I'll bet that fire was deliberately lit: they wanted Lily as hostage.'

'I know something about it, Matt. Jesse was here briefly a little while back. I removed a dozen or so buckshot pellets out of his upper arm. Not a severe wound, but no doubt awkward.' The medic paused

131

again to stare levelly at Ronan. 'He says a maverick they were branding kicked the fire into the brush – and he claims you killed Jack Ifield.'

'So that's why they left him at Lily's.' Ronan explained how the sheriff's body had been propped up against a log where it was sure to be found. 'Doc, I'll have to get moving and try to find this Redmount in the dark.'

By now Swanston was working on Barlow after his wife had cleaned up the wound. He spoke without looking up, probing.

'I have very good maps of the district – I use them when I make calls out to some of the more isolated ranches and farms. Dear, will you get my map case?' As his wife hurried towards the door, Swanston said, 'And better bring the brandy – I believe Matt could use a belt or two before he leaves.'

'I ain't gonna argue with you there, Doc, but I don't want to waste too much time. Barlow said Trace Burdin is mighty rough on women.'

'Yes,' Swanston said grimly, flatly – and there was a wealth of meaning in that short word. 'He likes to kill and maim – people or animals. When he goes hunting, he takes a shotgun, one barrel loaded with buckshot, the other with one of those Brenneke slugs. You know them?'

'The gunsmith told me about 'em. Twelve- or twenty-gauge solids that'll stop a grizzly in his tracks, and spread most of him over a good deal of the countryside doin' it.'

'Trace shoots anything that moves, wolves, big cats,

even a chipmunk, I've heard. Blows them apart, leaves them to die. That's the kind of man you're going up against, Matt.'

Ronan nodded, but didn't say anything.

They both knew he had no choice.

Doc Swanston's maps, made only five years earlier, were excellent – up to date and minutely detailed. The seemingly tireless medic finished doctoring Barlow and gave him an injection to ensure he'd get adequate rest. While Mrs Swanston arranged the wounded man in his infirmary bed, the doctor poured another round of brandy and they studied the map, eventually marking several places Doc figured would be suitable for ambush.

'If you approach so that you come up on the south-east slope of Redmount – it's only a glorified hill, by the way, like most of the so-called "mountains" up here: you need to go a little more east to find the big mountains and forests that few people associate with Kansas—' He stopped abruptly, seeming almost embarrassed. 'Ah, yes, there's a kind of ridge, about here – a low, notched affair. The regular trail is on the other side of it. But if you approach from this direction – I'll mark it with a cross – like so, then follow the natural lay of the ground to here – two crosses this time – you'll come to a clump of big rocks and be able to see much of the slope on the far side. As they say in the Army, you'll have the high ground. I'll sketch it for you.'

'It'll be pretty dark, Doc,' Ronan pointed out.

'Yes, so move quietly, and if anyone's waiting, they won't know you're there. Then, when you don't show on the regular trail, they're bound to grow impatient and—'

'Hopefully give away their position. Doc, I'm obliged to you again.'

'No need to feel that way. When someone like Trace Burdin is involved, I sometimes forget my Hippocratic Oath to only "heal and otherwise do good": I prefer to keep those things for people who deserve them.' He lifted his glass, lamplight sparkling through the dark amber liquid. 'The very best of luck to you, Matt – the *very* best! It doesn't make me happy to add that I think you'll need every ounce of it.'

Doc Swanston was right – dead right.

Ronan hired a fresh mount at the livery, a big black, which he thought was suitable, seeing as he would be riding mostly in the dark hours. It had long legs and powerful withers and had been well ridden locally.

But while the black may have been used to this broken country it had probably been on regular trails. Ronan was asking it to leave those trails and climb rugged slopes in the varying half-light of the late-rising moon. It gave him a little trouble but thankfully did not shrill or whinny in wild protest.

He hunkered down behind a big rock, struck a vesta to study the hand-drawn map Doc had made, and was just able to pick out the landmarks. It was a roundabout approach, long zigzags back and forth across the gradual rise.

His first attempt was way off, due to reading Doc's map wrong – he had inadvertently turned it around, oriented it north-south instead of east-west. He didn't realize it until he looked behind, saw the glint of the river and the light dancing from the flowing water, with the moon to his left.

After cursing himself for a fool, mildly panicked at losing all this time, and wondering what they were doing to Lily, he dug a little harder with his spurs and twigged the left ear of the horse when it insisted on turning the wrong way. Then the black must have recognized the country and with a snort that could have meant anything, bunched its muscles and carried him straight up to the rocky spine Doc had told him about. There were big boulders and clusters of smaller ones, an occasional clump of brush, all throwing shadows.

He let the horse have a blow in amongst the rocks, trailed the reins with a weighty rock on the ends, and climbed up between two large bouders, one half as big again as the other. He was sweating. His right hand ached and his fingers of his left were strained from pulling his entire weight up until he found a reasonably level place where he could stretch out and study the slope on the far side.

Here, Doc had figured, would be the best place for any ambush Denby and Burdin might set up. Ronan agreed.

Then his luck changed: the moon slid out from

behind a cloud and he saw the whole of the slope illuminated in pale silver light.

Not that it told him a hell of a lot, but he could make out the regular trail where an ambusher might expect a rider heading out from Skywater.

He found the shotgun something of a nuisance now, swinging as it was from the dog-swivel in the carry-loop Charlton had made. It was OK walking, but it had thudded relentlessly against his hip bone when riding and now was all but a damn nuisance as he tried to change position without having to get up from where he had stretched out.

Clank!

He froze: the damn weapon had banged against a rock. Moving nothing but his eyes, he strained to see as much of the slope as he was able. Nothing moved within the ambit of his vision but that had been a *noisy* clank. The night seemed very still and anyone waiting, listening for alien sounds surely must have heard it and wondered what metallic object had made it.

He would have to be dumb not to figure it out.

Ronan waited, hadn't moved a muscle since the clang, except to grab the weapon and hold it so it didn't swing and make another clank! He moved his head slowly, swore softly as the stiff hatbrim rasped across the rough surface of the rock that protected him. He froze again, unconsciously even holding his breath.

It was just as well he did: he heard something move, then, and he knew it was no animal.

In fact, it was almost an echo of the scraping sound his own hatbrim had made a few moments before. *And this was swiftly followed by the clatter of a dislodged stream of small stones . . . left and slightly below. . . .*

He lifted his body an inch, two, neck stretching as he strained to see where the sound could have come from.

And it almost cost him his life.

A shotgun thundered – which more than likely meant it was Trace Burdin. There was a heavy thud, a shattering sound, and hot lead sprayed across his neck and cheek. Something like a hurled rock whizzed past his ear. He knew then it *had* to be Burdin – that was a Brenneke slug that almost shattered the rock he lay behind. It was followed instantly by a charge of buckshot, but his instincts had cut in at super speed and he had thrust back, legs dropping over the rock shelf, helping to flatten his upper body as he tried to claw onto the rock. He heard the shot pellets whipping and buzzing as they fanned, ricocheting from boulder to boulder.

By the time he felt it safe to lift his head a little, the pale light catching his face, Burdin had reloaded with another slug.

When the shotgun fired, it made a heavier, thudding sound. Ronan rolled this time, dropping off the ledge and landing a couple of feet lower, once again breaking fingernails on his left hand as he tried to flatten.

The slug shattered and he felt lead rip through a loose section of his shirt, but it didn't touch his flesh.

137

He eased down to a ledge below. On the climb up he had noticed this small ledge with an opening made by two or three rocks with uneven surfaces, touching and hanging in space, locked together by their own weight and forming a ragged triangular peephole, twelve inches on each side.

He was badly cramped and stifled a moan as he moved his sore shoulder, scraping it across crumbling rock, trying to reach the pistol grip of his shotgun. Maybe if he was a contortionist it would have been easy but not with that crippled arm and the frozen hand. What he had to do was feed the gun back towards the hand, rather than try to force the clawed hand to the gun.

But it had to be done fast – he had actually figured this in seconds. turning his shoulders now, left hand swinging up the gun, easing it back to where his right forearm was jammed between his sweating body and the rock.

It made a noise, of course, and instantly Burdin triggered, but while the shot was quite accurate, the pellets flattened themselves against the rocks above him, whining and whistling away into the night: the overhang had protected him.

He used these sounds to work the slide under the barrel. His groping finger hooked around the trigger and depressed it. The gun went off before he expected but Burdin instinctively ducked, and in that time Ronan jerked the slide again, squirmed forward and even heard above the ringing in his ears the *click*! as Burdin snapped his breech closed, probably loading another slug. Moonlight streaked down a long, moving blued barrel, right where he had figured Trace had to be holed-up.

Now the dog swivel paid off.

Instead of having to lift the gun and move it into line, all he did was ease it on the swivel an inch or two so the barrel angled up – and shoot.

He didn't hear Burdin cry out but he saw the big body apparently leap from where he crouched, hit the rounded side of a rock and fall. It bounced off a smaller boulder and the shotgun slid away and tumbled between two rocks, the butt sticking up. He couldn't tell for sure from here but he thought the hammer was cocked.

Burdin was sprawled on his back, his spine bent like a bow from the pressure of a deadfall he had landed in. Just as Ronan straightened he heard the man groan sickly.

Matt fumbled and stumbled before he found reasonably secure footing, then made his way carefully around a rock, easing himself on to flatter ground. When he felt his boots on firm footing, he worked the shotgun slide again, made his way cautiously to where Burdin lay.

The man's face was pale in the wan light and his eyes watched Ronan approach. Matt was breathing heavily, stood over the barely conscious Burdin whose chest and right arm were shredded by buckshot. Ronan brought his gun across and placed the warm muzzle against Burdin's neck.

'Where is she?'

It took some time for him to figure out Burdin's reply but it was more or less what he expected. He nodded, and, making sure the dying man could see the movement, lifted the weapon and placed it against the killer's left leg which was bent at an odd angle only a couple of feet in front of where he stood.

'Die fast, or a little at a time, Burdin. No hammer on this to cock and make you jump. You'll only know what I'm doing when the gun goes off and takes your leg with it. You'll likely bleed to death anyway but I can produce a lot of pain to keep you company on your way to hell.'

Burdin said nothing but his stertorous breathing began to sound really ragged and his chest heaved. His lips parted and a little blood glistened as it spilled over.

'Or I can finish you quick with a six-gun – I've got one, or I can use yours. You got about three seconds to decide whether you want to shake hands with the Devil right away, or crawl there with bits and pieces falling off.'

Burdin didn't like that picture and he squirmed, making gargling noises in his throat.

Ronan's gun jumped a little and slid off the knee cap. 'Damn! This hand of mine's sure unreliable, almost jerked the trigger then. Can't stop the twitch once it starts, see? Oh-oh! No, it's OK, I thought it was going again, but you see how it is – the gun might go off without me even meaning it to. So once more: *where's Lily?*'

Burdin coughed and blood sprayed but there were also harsh sounds which Ronan tried to decipher and, by the time he had, Burdin was starting to thrash and cry out as his pain intensified.

Ronan poked him gently with his Colt barrel.

'Hey, Burdin? Can't heeeaarrr you!'

Moments later the single shot from a six-gun rang out and lost itself amongst the dark hills.

CHAPTER 14

A GOOD MAN

It had been an exhausting night for Matt Ronan.

The country was rugged, even though the hill wasn't big enough to call a 'small mountain'. Getting back to his horse turned out to be a major job: going down was harder than coming up. Steeper, too. Apparently he hadn't noticed when he had been driven by the urge to get to Lily.

And he still had no idea where she was – or even if she was still alive.

Trace Burdin had said only two words before he had died: '*Kill me!*'

And he had killed himself.

Ronan's pistol was cocked, pushed almost up against Burdin's face, as he had made his ultimatum: 'Talk or die'. Trace, in unbearable pain, had chosen to die. His right arm was shattered and useless but his left, though numbed and peppered with buckshot, was still useable – and Ronan hadn't realized this. Until, that is, Burdin swept the arm down against Matt's wrist and his thumb had jumped off the hammer, the muzzle a bare inch from Burdin's head. . . .

He had felt a rising panic after the first shock wore off: his only hope of finding Lily was now far beyond his reach. He didn't know the country. It was still mighty dark, despite the milky moonlight, and he was in a lot of pain himself. *Now, how the hell was he going to find her. . . ?*

He had to concentrate on getting back down the slope, using his right arm as little as possible. But he started one slide and the ground suddenly dropped away at a much steeper angle and he threw out his bad arm instinctively. He jarred it on a rock as he hurtled over the drop. The ground came up to meet him with a rush and then the night was filled with more and brighter stars than those above in the night sky.

He must have passed out. Not for long, hopefully, but when he came round fully, the fear of failure rushed in upon him like a tidal wave. He had plenty of pain in his right shoulder now and he concentrated on his main problem – finding Lily – using it as a distraction from his agony.

It worked, up to a point. His arm throbbed and ached but he crawled into an angle between some rocks, fumbled out Doc's map and struck a vesta. This position would shelter him from above, but not from directly in front, though that was one direction he figured he didn't have to worry about.

He and Doc had used the maps to mark the most likely places for ambush and Doc had also used his knowledge to indicate possible hiding places where Lily might be taken: caves, good campsites sheltered from bad weather – and a place called Dancey's Ridge.

'It's where Rawley Marks first set up his own small cabin – nothing more than a ten by ten shack of old clapboards ripped from demolished houses in town. The roof had caved in long ago, doors and shutters were stolen. Believe someone even broke down the chimney he'd made from river stones and carted 'em away.' Doc had paused, frowning. 'I'm sure it would be too obvious a place for Denby to use – still he's rat-smart.' Then he had shaken his head more decisively. 'No, Denby would choose somewhere closer to Delta C, I think. Somewhere he could run to easily in an emergency.'

Ronan had agreed, seeing as the place would not be secure for keeping a prisoner, either, but now . . . well, it wasn't all that much higher than the spot Burdin had chosen to bushwhack him.

Close enough for Denby to have heard the shooting? And what would he have deduced from it? Shotguns blasting the night apart . . . a long silence, then a single pistol shot.

He could decide either way: Burdin had wounded Ronan and finished him off with his six-gun, or, the other way round: Ronan had finished off Burdin. *Now what would happen?*

144

Denby would wait, sweating, rifle cocked, likely with Lily where he could reach her and use her to save his own neck if necessary, or, if the waiting got to him, he could make sure she was securely tied up and come looking to see just who was riding away from that ambush.

All this was supposing that Denby was using a double-bluff: the ridge and its derelict cabin would be naturally considered much too obvious a hiding place. Then again, that could be the very reason for using it!

Too apparent to be considered as a likely place to hold the Indian woman, so *use* it anyway. More than likely it would be passed up by whoever came looking and, of course, that would have to be Ronan, all supposing, of course, that he'd survived Burdin's ambush.

Matt decided to check out the ridge and its vandalized cabin before trying other likely places – the caves, for instance, over on the next rise; or a spring at the high end of a tiny box canyon Doc had somehow known about.

'So you got Trace!'

Ronan jumped, struggling half to his feet at the sound of the voice. Then Denby snapped:

'Stay put! Jesus, you are one tough bastard, ain't you?'

Ronan smiled thinly: he didn't mind being called that kind of a bastard. He froze as ordered and Denby stepped out from behind a bush growing at the base of a nearby rock that showed palely in the weird light. Denby held a rifle, cocked, of course, but it looked awkward the way he had it resting across the plaster cast over his right hand and lower forearm, left hand on the gooseneck, finger on the trigger.

'You sure left Trace in a mess. Saw him on the way down. Still, he's made bigger messes of men – and animals.'

'He killed himself, if you're interested.'

Denby arched his eyebrows. 'Yeah? How come?'

Ronan told him, stretching it a little, wanting to keep the man's mind off killing *him*. When he had finished Denby nodded.

'Hell, he's dead any way you look at it. Now it's your turn.'

The rifle muzzle lifted a couple of inches.

'You leave Lily in Marks' old shack?'

Denby's head snapped up. So Ronan knew about the place! *Dammit! He could have waited up there for him to show – but he hadn't so he had to make the most of it.*

'Don't really matter where I left her; she's no good to you now. Nor anyone else.' *Let Ronan figure out if that meant she was already dead!* 'We only took her so's you'd come after her. Had you picked as just that type of soppy Injun lover, see?'

'Don't you want to know what happened to Jesse?'

He saw Denby stiffen. The man's voice hardened a little. 'Jesse was all right when we quit the squaw's place.'

Ronan shrugged. 'We met soon after that.'

The silence stretched but Denby was right on edge now, alert: it was the wrong time for Ronan to make any kind of a move. He said nothing, knew Denby was examining his words, wondering if Matt was insinuating that he had killed Jesse during their meeting.

'Where you see Jesse?'

'Along the trail to town – when I was taking in Barlow to the sawbones.'

It was possible – and Denby knew it.

'Well? What happened?'

'Why don't you ask Jesse.'

'The hell're you playin' at. . . ?'

'He could be still breathin'.'

'By God, if you—'

'I didn't mean to shoot him.'

'*You shot him? With that goddamn thing you use?*'

Denby's voice cracked with rage and his rifle came up, spitting fire and smoke.

Ronan was moving before Denby had finished shouting his angry query – just a blur in the dark as he rolled to one side, taking him behind an egg-shaped boulder. Denby's bullet whined off and Matt grabbed at his six-gun in the cross draw holster – only it wasn't there.

He must have lost it on the slide down that steep slope that had caught him unawares. . . .

Denby's lever hadn't clashed as he reloaded! The fact stabbed into Ronan's mind as he fought to get his leg under him so he could make at least some sort of attempt to escape Cline's next shot.

But Denby was in such a rage that he was no longer functioning properly: his timing was out. He

147

tried to jerk the lever in a one-hand-throw, which is quite possible, but only when a man has worked at perfecting it, and Denby was not one of those men. So the lever only half-closed – around Denby's fingers when he didn't get them out of the way soon enough. He yelled, *screamed*, in a mad rage, dropping the rifle.

Then Ronan came hurtling across the short space, bent almost double, turning slightly to protect his damaged shoulder, left hand cocked in a well-remembered postion to smash a man's jaw. He didn't have the power behind it now that he had had when working for the travelling tent show, but it was enough to snap Denby's head around and send him sprawling against a rock. He clawed at it, yelled in pain as his mangled hand jammed between his body and the boulder.

The agony itself snapped his muscles and tendons into a violent movement away from the rock. Matt's body crashed into him. They were jammed in a tight space between the close-set rocks, both grunting and heaving off the other in their efforts to straighten. Both lurched away at approximately the same time, Ronan a split second ahead of Denby.

Cline twisted away from the expected punch but Matt's right side was facing him, so he could not use that arm. But Denby was quick as a snake – saw his advantage and drove a hammer blow with his left fist against Ronan's shoulder. Matt groaned and went down to one knee. Denby lifted his own knee into his face and stretched Ronan out on the slope.

Teeth bared, Cline jumped with both feet aimed at Matt's head. Ronan spun away but felt the wind of Denby's boots against his face. He kept rolling away and slid on to a level piece of ground. It enabled him to dig in his boot heels and his own impetus helped him come upright. He bent his left arm and Cline actually ran on to the point of his elbow with his left eye, like a driven spike.

Denby yelled and staggered off to one side. Matt went after him, trying to keep from instinctively using both arms as he would have in a prize fight – like following the straight left with a right hook, then the left again in the midriff, and finishing the man off with an upper cut.

Those moves were denied him because of his injuries – but they were also denied Denby Cline. And Cline had an advantage: his crippled hand was almost entirely encased in hard-set plaster, only half the fingers free. He swung that arm, the weight of the plaster adding to its impetus and power, grunting with the effort.

Ronan saw it coming and dropped flat, hurting, but kicking up to his shoulders and bringing both boots crashing into Denby's chest. With Cline's impetus added it folded Ronan's knees up almost to his face. Denby spilled off the boots, hit a rock and slid off. Dazed, he lay there and watched Ronan stagger upright. Then Denby got his knees under him and hurled his crouching body forward like a missile.

He crashed into Matt's legs, wound his good arm

around them and twisted violently. Ronan had no choice but to go with the pressure and he started to tumble over Cline. Almost past the point of balance, he managed to get a knee against the side of Cline's head, crushing it against the rock briefly, but long enough to tear at an ear and make the blood flow. Denby screamed obscenities.

Matt had to go with the fall anyway, sprawled, caught his crippled hand on a rock and smothered a curse, figuring he would need all of his breath.

He did: Denby, bloody-faced, almost crying with rage and frustration, was getting up off his knees and dragging his six-gun from his belt: he hadn't bothered with a holster after his gun hand had been injured.

Matt didn't know where he found the energy or the effort to react as he did, but he flung himself behind the bush growing at the base of the rock, bent back a whippy branch and let fly as Denby finally found balance and levelled the six-gun. The branch slashed across Denby's bleeding face and knocked him staggering. The Colt blasted into the ground and Matt got his legs pounding, driving him towards the shotgun he had dropped.

By God, I'll pay for this! The strange but appropriate thought flashed through his head as the slide *click-clacked* and thrust a shell into the breech. He automatically depressed the trigger and the gun bucked against his straining wrist. Denby Cline was hurled back at least a yard, feet clear of the ground. There was a sodden thud, like a sack of corn dropping from a barn roof and Denby's body was jerked forward as if by a rope.

He landed face down in the dirt and lay there, unmoving. . . .

By then, Ronan had slid another shell along the loading tube into the breech, but held his finger pressure on the trigger just in time. He figured another blast wasn't necessary.

Denby wasn't dead, though he was badly hit on the right side, some smashed ribs exposed and clothes and flesh torn away. Ronan's head was spinning. His legs would barely hold him. He lowered the smoking shotgun and sagged to the ground, leaning back against a rock, his gun falling a foot away from b is a his left leg. He closed his eyes, fighting for breath.

But they snapped open as, barely recognizing Denby's pain-filled voice, Cline said, 'D-die, you—'

There was a pistol shot and Ronan's body stiffened, instinctively tensing to take the impact of the bullet.

Nothing happened.

The gunsmoke cleared slowly and he saw a blurred sight he didn't believe: Denby Cline was down on his side, bleeding from a bullet wound high up on the left side of his chest, blood flooding.

Wearily and blearily, Matt swung his gaze around to his right, having to twist his neck a little, and saw the cloud of gunsmoke drifting through the bush.

Standing beside the bush was Water Lily Marks, a Colt pistol held in both hands, which were bleeding. Her forearms were scraped raw, the sleeves of her buckskin jacket hanging in tatters.

He jerked up straighter as he saw blood all around her mouth, too.

'You o-kay now, Ro-nan,' she said huskily and her legs folded as she pitched forward.

He was far too slow to catch her and she hit the ground on her right side, the gun falling from her loose grip.

It seemed that the world was seven steps removed from where he was. His brain was buzzing, pain knifed through most of his upper body, and he felt queasy. It was just as if he had been in a twenty-round fight where the only acceptable ending was when only one man was left standing.

If he recalled correctly he had fought three such fights, but that was a long time ago, a long – time – ago, and—

He felt heat on his face and down his upper body and he thought, *I'm at the Gates of Hell!*

His eyes flew open and he almost choked trying to get a breath, head swirling. His upper body sagged as he had a blurred vision of a fire and shadows moving between it and himself. *Which one's Old Nick?* he wondered as a big form towered over him.

Then he realized he was looking at muddy, run-over riding boots, such as you could see on any ranny in cattle country. He raised his eyes slowly as a voice asked,

'You comin' to join us, feller?'

Asking? 'Do – do I have a choice?'

'Well, hell, I guess so! Hey, you hear that? Wants to know if he has a choice of joinin' us!'

'Still half outta his head. Give him a shot, Mort.'

Matt Ronan felt the cold lip of a bottle pushed into his mouth and then the burning liquor and he coughed and spluttered and hawked and his eyes at last came into focus and he saw the group of grinning men squatting around a camp-fire.

It did nothing to help him get his wits about him, but when he moved his head and saw Denby Cline's shot-torn body lying half covered by a worn saddle-blanket, he started to remember. His left hand suddenly closed into a fist; his right tried to join it but without success, the rush of pain helping to clear his head. He looked around quickly.

'Where is she? Water Lily. . . ?'

The big man who had been standing over him, squatted and handed him a burning cigarette, held it so he could take a drag.

'You mean the squaw? They took her back to town – she needs a doctor. Figure you do, too.'

'Yeah, not feelin' too chipper. Who're you?'

'Nelson's the name, Mort Nelson. I run a freight line out from Dodge. Some judge, O'Malley, grabbed me and a few of my boys in Skywater and said he had authority to deputize us to go lookin' for a body at a burned-out cabin. We was to bring it in and scout around and look for two fellers with their right arms busted up and in slings or bandages and, well, you qualify. And the other's over there under the saddle-blanket, but he ain't in a talkin' mood any more.'

153

Trying to absorb this information, Ronan said, 'Sounds like he did some talkin' already.'

'Yeah, shot to hell, dyin'. Wanted to clear his conscience I reckon. Dunno what he was meanin', but he said tell Ringo? Rogan? Some name like that—'

'Ronan?' Matt gasped.

'Yeah! That's it, tell Ronan it was Jesse killed Jack. You make any sense outta that?'

Matt nodded, even half-smiled. 'The girl, she all right?' Nelson stared at him strangely. 'Last I recollect of her she was bloody round the mouth and her hands.'

'Oh, yeah. Seems she was tied up and, well, someone didn't treat her like a lady, but she chewed through her gag, then went to work on the rawhide they'd tied round her wrists. Mighty strong damn teeth, them squaws. Come from chewing buffalo hides to make 'em soft, I guess.'

'Usually deer hide,' Ronan corrected him. 'Thank God she's OK. I—'

Then suddenly he toppled forward into impenetrable darkness, falling, falling. *By Godfrey, it was a helluva long way down!*

He was no longer conscious when he hit bottom.

'Aw, no! Not again!'

He opened his eyes and saw that he was propped up on a bed in Doc Swanston's infirmary. His mind felt clear and he couldn't believe he was back where he started – or almost.

'What did he say?' someone asked.

'Don't you savvy good American? I said "Aw, no!" I can't believe I'm here again.'

He blinked and looked around him. Actually he wasn't in the infirmary, but he recognized the room. It was the one Doc used after he had operated on someone – the recovery room, that's what it was called! Somewhere the chloroform could wear off and the patient could get his wits about him once more.

'We savvy your lingo, Matt. Here, take this. Your speech is slurred and I think you need a drink.'

The doctor held a glass of lemon juice with a touch of brandy in it to his lips. He gulped greedily, grabbing the medic's hand when he tried to take the glass away.

'Easy! Don't gulp or you'll be throwing up and I assure you my wife will not be happy. She's getting all dolled up for her evening at the ladies' quilting group.'

Ronan reluctantly stopped drinking: his throat and gullet felt much better now. 'Well, I hope she has a nice evening. Doc, what in hell's happened to me?'

'We picked up some from your ravings under the chloroform. I had to reset your shoulder; it's going to be sore for quite some time but you won't need to stay here if you don't want.'

'I don't want! Er, no offence, Doc, but I've had a bellyful of places like this.'

The medic raised a hand. 'Understandable. You know Seamus O'Malley deputized a bunch of freighters to bring in Jack Ifield's body? Yes. Well, they found Lily wandering in the hills, trying to get help to bring you in. Well, let's just cut it short and say here you are.'

'How about Lily?'

'She can tell you herself in a few minutes.' He lowered his voice. 'She's helping the wife get into a new set of corsets – giving her a waist I can put my hands around, fingers and thumbs touching.'

'You're an old lecher, Doc! You surprise me.'

'Surprise myself at time. Er, touching on a related subject – sort of – you'll be pleased to know I'm almost certain Lily's baby will be born naturally. They gave her a rough time, but mostly it was a beating. Someone did . . . try to violate her, but, well, as I say, I'm almost certain the birth will go quite normally.'

'Almost?'

'I'm not a a clairvoyant, Matt, but I do know my medicine and I know Lily's strength, both physical and mental. So, once again, I say, I *believe* the birth will be normal.'

'All right, Doc, all right! Judas, I didn't mean to criticize you as a medic. I'm mighty glad to hear she'll have some part of this Rawley Marks she was in love with to nurture and take care of.'

Swanston stared at him. 'You know, Matt, that's a very touching thought. There are not many men in this country who would see that side of it.'

'No, they just think she's a whore. *And* I'll bet there's more than a mite of jealousy involved.'

Just then Lily came in and Ronan had to compose his face when he saw the puffy mouth, the bruises around her eyes and the way she moved, hugging one arm against her side.

He smiled at her. 'You look pretty good in white women's clothes.'

She smiled a little and held the dark green skirt away from her legs. She wore a white linen blouse with a dark green scarf around her neck – he thought he could see the darkening purple of bruises just above the silk. There was a black cummerbund around her slim waist, though it likely wasn't quite as slim as a few months previously.

'I owe you my life.'

'Den-by die any-way.'

'Yeah, but he died because you shot him and saved me.'

'You call it . . . squared?'

' "Square". Yeah, OK.' He chuckled. 'Gonna have to teach you to speak better.'

'You understand – that enough.'

'Yeah.' He lowered his voice, serious now. 'You really all right, Lily? Doc says they didn't do too much harm.'

She waved a hand disdainfully. 'Bur-din more sore than me.'

His smile widened again. 'You mean you managed to. . . ?'

She arched her eyebrows and nodded, smiling. 'He walk funny after.'

'Wish I'd been able to see it.'

'You busy.'

'Huh? Oh, yeah, I was trying to find you. Barlow!

157

Hell, I just remembered him! Is he OK, Doc? You were going to operate.'

'You'll have his company while you recover. Yes, he's tough, we decided earlier, though getting on in years, so it'll take a little time.'

'Did O'Malley accept Nelson's word that Denby said Jesse killed Jack Ifield?'

'Yes. It was substantiated by one of Delta's cowhands Barlow had wounded during the attack at the cabin. Jesse's been arrested and it looks like he'll either spend the rest of his life on the rockpile or dangle from a noose.'

'Reckon he'd prefer the noose.'

'Yes, so do I, now he's lost both sons.' The doc straightened, saying, 'I'll leave you two for now,' then went out quickly. Suddenly there seemed to be an awkwardness between Ronan and Lily.

She sat tentatively on the end of his bed.

'You go away when better?'

'We-ell, figured I might try to do somethin' with your cabin. There'll be some of it still standing. I'm not all that good with tools, and now,' he indicated his crippled hand. 'But I figure I could get the place liveable in time – for you and the baby.'

'Oh, Ro-nan. You cannot! You have your life.'

'Thanks to you. No, Lily, I'd be mighty pleased to be able to do something for you. Pretty sure Barlow would help, too. He says he builds a mean riverstone fireplace.'

After a while she lifted her face and looked steadily at him. 'You good man, Ro-nan.'

He lowered his gaze. 'Lily, I never knew my father, nor anyone I could sort of replace him with. Barlow's come closest if you want to know, but I – I sure wouldn't like your son – or daughter – to have to go through life without knowing someone they could consider as a – a father substitute. I mean, Marks is dead and . . . I wouldn't *be* their real father but I'd sort of hang around if you—'

'It will be son. He will call you "Uncle".'

Ronan's mouth dropped open and then he smiled again.

'Hell, that's a good idea! But it's up to you, I mean—'

'I know what you mean. I tell you again: You good man, Ro-nan.'

He was suddenly very tired and stifled a yawn.

It seemed a nice thought to go to sleep with.